Gwen

Gwen

by

CAROLYN POGUE

SUMACH
PRESS

Library and Archives Canada Cataloguing in Publication

Pogue, Carolyn, 1948–
Gwen : a young adult novel / Carolyn Pogue

ISBN 978-1-894549-80-6

I. Title.

PS8581.O2257 G94 2009   jC813'.54   C2009-900280-9

Edited by Jennifer Day
Cover & Design by Liz Martin

Front cover portrait: Gladys Gwendoline Parsons,
1898, photographer unknown.

Chapter 11 appeared in a slightly different version in *Beginnings:
Stories of Canada's Past,* ed. Ann Walsh, Ronsdale Press, 2001.

*Sumach Press acknowledges the support of the Canada Council
for the Arts and the Ontario Arts Council for our publishing program.
We acknowledge the financial support of the Government of Canada
through the Book Publishing Industry Development Program
(BPIDP) for our publishing activities.*

ONTARIO ARTS COUNCIL
CONSEIL DES ARTS DE L'ONTARIO

Printed and bound in Canada

Published by
SUMACH PRESS
1415 Bathurst Street #202
Toronto ON Canada M5R 3H8

*info @sumachpress.com
www.sumachpress.com*

Mixed Sources
Product group from well-managed
forests, controlled sources and
recycled wood or fiber
www.fsc.org Cert no. SW-COC-002358
© 1996 Forest Stewardship Council
FSC

98%

ANCIENT FOREST ™
FRIENDLY

Acknowledgements

Nia:wen and thank you to:

Paula Whitlow, Chiefswood National Historic Site,
Ohsweken, Ontario

Dave Lorente, Home Children Canada, Renfrew, Ontario
Derek Warren, Aftercare Department,
Barnardo's Headquarters, London, England

And – Andrea Czarnecki, Reverend Bill Phipps,
Lynn Matthison, Gail Sidonie Sobat, Ann Walsh,
Barbara Sinclair Shoomski, Reverend Barry Pridham,
Donna McPhee, Nina Burnham, James Pogue,
John and Thea Patterson at Abbey North,
Jennifer Day at Sumach Press.

*The story is dedicated to the memories of
my grandmother, Gladys Gwendoline,
and to poet, performer and pathfinder
E. Pauline Johnson.*

Dear Reader,

I always knew that my grandmother had come from England to Canada. What I didn't know, until I was grown up, was that she had been a Home Child. In 1898, she had come to work as a servant when she was ten years old. Knowing this made me admire her even more. It also made me want to write a story that would honour her and other brave, imaginative children.

Some of this story is true; much of it is made up. I have modelled Dr. Allan on Dr. Thomas Barnardo, a real person who cared for children in England who were homeless, abandoned or starving. Through him and two notable women named Maria Rye and Annie MacPherson, as well as other childcare workers of the times, about 100,000 children were housed, trained to work and sent to Canada. Some children were sent to Australia, Africa and New Zealand, too.

Barnardo and others also established Ragged Schools, where ragged-clothed street children were given a bowl of soup and could learn reading, writing, arithmetic and study the Bible. Today you can visit the website of the Ragged School Museum of Copperfield Road in London, England.

There are several books for young people and adults about Home Children in Canada, and the Home Children Canada Society helps people trace their history. In Britain, Barnardo's is still working for kids, although in very different ways than a century ago.

E. Pauline Johnson was a Mohawk writer, poet and performer who dazzled audiences in Canada, the US and England. Her original stage costumes reflected her Native and non-Native heritage. These are facts. I did change one fact of Ms Johnson's life so that it would fit the story better: when Pauline Johnson went to London in 1894, she performed in the parlours of fashionable people. It was actually on her second trip, in 1906, that she performed in the Steinway Theatre. You can find books for all ages about her life and writings on the Internet, in bookstores and in libraries. Author Margaret Atwood has written the story for an opera about Pauline Johnson's life.

E. Pauline Johnson was also a pathfinder. In a time when women were considered second class citizens, she was first class. She made her living from her writing and performances. She was the first Canadian writer to *write* Canada, coast to coast. Today, you can visit the website of Chiefswood, her childhood home. It is now a national historic site open to visitors, owned and operated by the Six Nations of the Grand River Territory. It is near Brantford, Ontario.

I wrote this story to honour adult and child pathfinders from our history whose examples help us to break new trails today. *Gwen* is a fictional story.

— *Carolyn Pogue,*
JANUARY 2009

Prologue

LONDON, 1894

DAD'S SNORING WAS THE FIRST THING I HEARD ON MY TENTH birthday. Usually he sounded like a cart rumbling down the cobbles, but this day his snoring was soft as an old tom's purr.

I dressed quickly and took money from the tea caddie on the shelf. Closing the door ever so quietly, I tiptoed downstairs and went out into the early morning fog. At the shops I bought two buns and some new tea. The other tea was so worn out I could hardly taste it.

When Dad woke up, I had the fire ready and we toasted buns and had fresh tea and I scraped the bottom of the jar for the last of the jam and it was lovely. He said, "Gwen Peters, this is a real celebration!" and I said, "It's my birthday." He was quiet a moment. "Then today is the day I'll take you in back and we'll have a look at Miss Pauline Johnson from Canada, mark my words. Miss Johnson is a real Indian princess. Only you have to make yourself very small, Gwen Peters, because it'll be a sad day if I'm found out. We'll have not a shilling in the house if I lose this job." Dad had been working as a cleaner at the theatre for four whole months. For him, that was a long time.

After our tea, Dad pulled on his shirt, snapped his suspenders, stood up straight and made a deep bow. "I'd be honoured, m'lady," he said in his best gentleman's voice, "if you would accompany me to the theatre, for you are the fairest young lady in all of London." I curtsied and gave him my hand. "'Twould be a pleasure, Sir," I said. And then he went along to the pub and I went down to the pump in the courtyard. Tim was there, washing his face. Tim lived on the street, even though Dad said he could live with us. He stayed around our street because people looked out for him and gave him a meal or a scarf sometimes. Tim and me had been friends for ages. He was teaching me to read. "Hey!" he yelled, "what are you smiling at?" I told him I was going to the theatre. "Luck-ee!" he crowed. It was nice to think he was glad for me. I carried the water upstairs and washed up the cups in the tin bucket.

I was beside myself all day long. I couldn't think how to make the hours fly faster; the hands of the clock seemed stuck. It was no use looking for Tim again, because this was the day he went to the Ragged School to get a bowl of soup and learn his sums and how to read books. I was desperate enough that I went over to old Mrs. Bostwick's in the next flat and told her I'd do an errand for her. She sent me off to the greengrocer's for some cabbage, but it didn't take near long enough.

I washed my hair and even used a little coal to warm the water because it was my birthday and I felt like it. I cleaned my boots so hard I made the hole in the side a little bigger and I couldn't think how to fix it. I broke a needle trying to sew it, so I took it to Mrs. Bostwick. She just shook her head and said, "Them boots is done for, child." When I told her I was going to the theatre to see the Indian from Canada she said he likely wouldn't be wearing shoes anyway so I'd be right at home. I told her that this Indian was Pauline Johnson, a famous performer at the theatre. She frowned. Mrs. Bostwick knows how to make bread dough and jam, but she doesn't know a thing about the theatre or plays. She says it's all lies and against the Bible.

"The Good Book says not to lie. Theatre is all lies, girl!" She rocked in her chair, shoved her huge body around a little, and looked at me hard.

"I try not to interfere with how you're being raised up, poor motherless child, but it's not right. Your poor mum was a Bible-readin' woman. Your dad's got to find a Christian woman to marry. Quick! Before you're lost forever to Satan!"

Sometimes I have the patience to listen to her for a while, but not today. She shouldn't be telling me stuff like that. It's not right. My dad can't help that Mom died and he can't help that he likes to take a few nips of gin to get him through the long days and nights. And I can't help that when she gave me an old dress to wear I did the wrong thing. How was I to know she'd be mad that I cut it up to make a princess costume for a play?

Anyway, I can look after things, and the rent for our rooms is paid most times, and I don't need someone like Mrs. Bostwick to tell me that silly Satan stuff. I'd like to tell her to shut her gob. Instead I tell her I have to go and wash out my stockings.

When I went back to our flat I wrapped a piece of string right around my boot and tied it tight and rubbed a piece of coal over it. You could hardly see the string at all.

I couldn't believe how lucky I was to go to the theatre to see a real performance. Dad told me all about the bright lights and audiences dressed up like kings and queens. When I go to help Dad home at night, the performances have ended because I go after he's finished sweeping up and putting away all the stuff the people use there. I love the smell of the greasepaint.

Once I peeked in a back room and saw the costumes and there were feathers and silk and lace and fans — magic stuff. That's where I got the idea to ask Dad for the bits I have in my costume box. I have 43 feathers now and soon I'll have enough to make a real boa like the ladies use.

Finally the day ended. I went along with Dad just as the men were lighting the street lamps. Dad helped me to read the hard words on the sign at the front of the theatre: "Miss E. Pauline Johnson (Tekahionwake) in her Unique and Refined Recitals of her Own Works — Canada's Foremost Comedienne and Poetess — Pathetic — Dramatic — Patriotic. Endorse and Applaud Her!" On it was her picture with her arms right up and looking for all the world like a star. We went around to the back of the theatre, and entered the door marked "Stage."

Inside, Dad told me to be very small and not say a word and I didn't. I stood in the shadows near where they keep the brooms and mops, still as a statue. I could hear people talking down the hallways and smell all the powder and paint the ladies use. When someone came hurrying by I didn't even breathe. After a while my eyes got used to the dark and I saw a sad little man sitting by the curtains, just staring at the floor. If I worked in the theatre, I wouldn't stare at the floor, I'd be looking all around and listening. But then, if I worked in the theatre I'd be busy in a dressing room somewhere straightening my feathers and putting paint on my face and being beautiful.

A big fat man with spectacles and huge eyebrows came rushing by me and I sucked in my breath and pretended I wasn't there. "Anyone out there?" he asked the sad little man. The curtain man stood up and peeked through the curtains. "Full house, Sir," he said. Spectacles rushed away down the hall. I could hear him calling, "Miss Johnson? Are you ready?" Suddenly, she was there.

She was wearing a blue hat with feathers, and a blue dress made of silk that rustled when she walked. She even had blue shoes. She was the most beautiful lady I've ever seen in my life. I tugged Dad's sleeve and we moved through the shadows to where the curtain man stood. He didn't even notice, he was staring so hard at Miss Johnson. I couldn't see the audience, but I could hear them. They sounded like the ocean waves, or anyway what I think the ocean waves would sound like.

The sad man pulled the curtains suddenly, and Miss Johnson walked to the centre of the stage. The lights were blinding and hot. The audience went silent, like suddenly they'd disappeared. And she stood there with all those eyes looking at her and she lifted her head, proud, and when she opened her mouth and spoke I thought my heart would fly out of my chest; I thought she would be able to hear it beating.

She took a deep breath and began with a poem about paddling in a canoe. Canoes are boats they have over in Canada. The poem was called "In the Shadows." She made the words dance and sway; I never heard such pretty words:

I am sailing to the leeward,
Where the current runs to seaward
  Soft and slow,
Where the sleeping river grasses
Brush my paddle as it passes
  To and fro.

She was like a magic queen, she was, and made us *see* the land of the silver birch and the "rushes on the river's rim ..." Miss Pauline Johnson had all the words in her head, so she didn't need papers. Her arms were free to move like the river grasses and show how to paddle down the river.

After the audience clapped their hands off, she said a poem about two people in a canoe who just float, float, float on a river, happy as anything. Miss Johnson stepped toward the audience, bent toward them. The lights dimmed and she wrapped the room in softness.

The river, deep and still,
The maple-mantled hill,
The little yellow beach whereon we lie,
The puffs of heated breeze,
All sweetly whisper — These

Are days that only come in a Canadian July.

She stepped back slowly, raised her eyes to a pretend sun, and raised her arm to it.

So, silently we two
Lounge in our still canoe
Nor fate, nor fortune matters to us now:
So long as we alone
May call this dream our own,
The breeze may die, the sail may droop, we care not when
or how.

Miss Pauline Johnson put her arms behind her head and slowly turned around, her blue silk dress swirled about her, like she herself was in the river. Beautiful.

After some pretty love poems I thought it was all over, but Dad said, "No, there's more after the intermission." I wouldn't have believed it, but after a little while she did come back. This time her dress was even more marvelous, brilliant white, made of soft leather. It had fringes all around and white fur at the top. There was red at the neck and bottom, and big round silver pins caught the stage light like suns flashing. She wore a great red robe draped down her back, and a necklace made from bear claws. Her hair was wild and soft without any hair pins. Two long feathers were tied into it at the back. She stood like a queen in the centre of the stage.

Next she said a poem about a man named Wolverine who saved a trapper from a terrible death. Now everything changed. Miss Johnson stepped toward the audience, bent toward them. The lights dimmed. It was a little bit scary.

Wolverine began:

"Yes, sir, it's quite a story though you won't believe it's true,
But such things happened often when I lived beyond the Soo."
And the trapper tilted back his chair and filled his
   pipe anew.

She leaned back, pretending to hold a pipe …

"One day I had been settin' traps along a bit of wood,
An' night was catchin' up to me jest faster 'an it should,
When all at once I heard a sound that curdled up my blood."

Miss Pauline Johnson put her head back and howled. The
hairs on the back of my neck stood straight up. I squeezed
Dad's hand and held my breath.

"It was the howl of famished wolves — I didn't stop to think,
But jest lit out across for home as quick as you could wink,
But when I reached the river's edge I brought up at the brink.

"That mornin' I had crossed the stream straight on a sheet
   of ice
An' now, God help me! There it was, churned up
   an' cracked to dice …"

What happened is that the trapper got trapped and he
was going to die except Wolverine came to save him and
some people didn't know that Wolverine was a hero; they
thought he was a thief and they *shot* him.

The theatre was dead silent. The little man by the curtains
kept his eyes, big as saucers, on Miss Johnson. I held Dad's
warm hand, there in the dark by the brooms and mops. Then
Miss Johnson carried us away again, over the ocean and into
Canada where the wolves will *snap* your bones and the rivers

choke with ice.

Next was a poem she called "A Cry from an Indian Wife." It is a story about a lady who doesn't want her husband to fight, but what can she do? And she doesn't want the soldiers' mothers to be sad, either. And it's sad and terrible and wonderful and Miss Johnson moved wild across that stage. She bent and waved and yelled and whispered. She painted pictures in the air, and carried us away from London. We were *with* her on the prairie when she cursed "the war that drinks their harmless blood!" There could not have been one person in the audience or behind the stage who was not riding, paddling, walking with her. It made the little hairs on my neck and arms stand straight up in the air.

Dad was hardly drunk afterwards. I helped him with the sweeping up after everyone had left and I was quiet as a mouse. I didn't have to help him home hardly at all and when we got there I lay down on my blanket and pretended I was on the ground with my horse and canoe nearby. I could hear Miss Johnson's words for the longest time. It was hard to sleep. It was the best birthday ever.

I lay there dreaming that when I grew up I'd be an actor and stand on the stage like Miss Johnson and the audience would love me. I knew I could be a poet, too. I already had a beautiful poem about my mother up in heaven that I kept safe, every word, in my head. I made a solemn pledge to heaven that night that I would practise every single day the letters Tim taught me from his lessons at the Ragged School, so I could write my poems out and look at them. I went to sleep conjuring up a new play for Tim and me to do. When I become Miss Pauline Johnson for him, he'll be amazed.

Chapter One

MY ELEVENTH BIRTHDAY, 1895

THE DAY I TURNED ELEVEN I WOKE UP EARLY BECAUSE OF Dad's cough. I even forgot it was my birthday for a while; I was too busy lighting the fire quick, quick to make Dad some tea so he could breathe better. I put some old blankets and coats behind his back so he could sit up a little.

After tea, he said, "Happy Birthday, Gwen Peters!" and coughed more and spit into the bucket. Then he reached under the mattress and gave me a book: *The White Wampum* by Pauline Johnson. In the front he'd written, "To Gwen: Stories will carry you through. Remembering a great lady. Love, Dad." It was beautiful, with a hard brown cover that said *The White Wampum* and *Pauline Johnson* and *The Bodley Head* right on it. On the front was an axe-looking thing with a belt draped on it and a word: *Tekahionwake.* Inside was a picture of mountains and a camp and teepees that made you want to go right in there, by the fire. The book must have cost a great deal of money. I could hardly speak when he gave it to me.

"I was saving up for a new dress for you, Gwen," he said, "but I thought another patch wouldn't hurt your old one, and you love Miss Johnson so." And that's all he could say because the coughing started again so bad.

When I emptied his coughing bucket I saw there was a lot of blood. There was no time for my lovely gift. I had to run over to Mrs. Bostwick's 'cause she told me if there was more blood we had to do something. She came right away.

"What's this? What's this?" she said, like she was mad at him. Like he's been coughing like that on purpose. "What's to be done now?" she asked. But Dad didn't answer. He just lay there, looking gray and sad. Mrs. Bostwick told me to find Tim and send him for a doctor. When I came back, Dad was asleep again.

After the doctor left, Mrs. Bostwick called me into her flat.

"When did he go to work last?" she asked.

"Last week," I said. He's been too tired lately.

Mrs. Bostwick rocked in her chair a moment and then asked what I planned to do in the future. I didn't know what she meant. And then she told me.

"He's not going to get better, Gwen," she said. "You need to make a plan." I was so stunned I didn't say a word. "Do you have people?" she asked. "Aunts or uncles? Anybody?"

I told her she was a fat cow and she shouldn't talk like that. "I'll get him better!" I said. "And if you were any kind of Christian woman you'd help me instead of scaring me out of my wits!" I walked out of her flat and slammed the door as hard as I could to make her sorry.

I didn't want to cry in front of Dad, so I raced down the

stairs, out onto the street and ran and ran and ran for a long time. Then I sat in the market for a while and watched the flower sellers. A flower dropped from a bundle on a cart. I picked it up and it made me feel ever so calm and lovely just to smell that soft pink rose. I imagined I was in the countryside where roses grow in rich people's gardens, where there's a nice house and a little brook for me and Tim to look at, or maybe a park like where I went once when Mum was alive. After a while I decided that Mrs. Bostwick really was a cow and even though I'd never actually seen one, I thought that they must look like her and then I felt better. I bought a sausage to build up my dad's strength and started for home, walking slowly this time. I didn't want to hurry back. I looked through the crowds for Tim. No matter what was going on, it was always better with him.

Tim was my true friend because when I had conjured up a play and needed someone to be the ogre or the bad guy, Tim would always do it. I had a proper gentleman's hat that I found on the street one day. I kept it in my costume box and if I let him wear that hat he'd be anyone I'd say. I'd wear the feather boa with 138 feathers sewn on a piece of pretty red cloth for when I became a grand lady. Sometimes I was Pauline Johnson and I didn't need anyone, except to pull the curtain, which was an old sheet on the clothesline out back. Other times I'd be a poor girl who needed to be saved. Some days I didn't need anyone to save me so I wouldn't let Tim play at all, but he'd stay to be the audience.

Some days Tim told stories from his book at the Ragged School and I told him how we could make it into a play and then we did. When my dad watched he always yelled "encore" and "bravo" because he said that's what they yell at the theatre when the show was fantastic, and we *were*. Sometimes Dad made up a story for us and we did that, too. Sometimes he'd tell us about the stories that Mr. Gilbert and Mr. Sullivan would do at the theatre, so then we'd do one of those. Once even Mrs. Bostwick told me a story, about Delilah and Samson from the Bible. It was such a good story that I invited her to our show, but she went into a big speech about plays being wicked, so after that I didn't invite her again.

Tim said when he grew up he'd be an actor too, and people would pay money to see us perform in the theatre.

I couldn't see him anywhere so I stopped looking when I almost stepped right into a hot pile of bleedin' horse droppings. I hopped over it and bumped right into someone who almost knocked me over. He caught me by the arm. "Hey Gwen! Close call!" It was Tim!

"Bloody hell!" I swore.

"You alright, then? What are you doing, dreaming up another play?"

Suddenly I felt very, very tired. "No, Tim," I said. "And I … I can't play today. I have to think."

Tim was my true friend, because he didn't ask any more or bother me after that. He just walked with me and didn't say a word. After we'd walked a bit he disappeared for a minute and came back with an apple and stuck it in my pocket.

When I got back to our flat Mrs. Bostwick was there. I told her, "I want to be alone," and she said, "There's no harm in that, I guess, but I'll be back in an hour to check on him."

I cut up the apple for us both, but Dad was even more gray and he had coughed more blood and he wouldn't eat. I sat on the floor by the mattress and held his hand. It was cold. The only sounds were the pigeons cooing on the window ledge and Dad's rattling breath. Suddenly, the pigeons flew off. It took a moment to realize that there was no other sound in the room at all. Dad was silent.

I tried to warm up his hand by rubbing and rubbing it. I wanted to shake him, to scream at him, "Dad! Wake up! Don't leave me here all by myself on my birthday!" But I didn't. I felt like I was turned to stone.

Mrs. Bostwick had said she'd be back in an hour. What would she do now? Send me to the workhouse where the rats and fleas bite holes in you and the people are half starved and there are no plays or books or singing? Throw me on the street to beg?

I put Dad's hand on his silent chest and gathered up my coat, my other dress, my costumes and made a bundle out of them. I checked the tea caddie for money — three shillings.

Mrs. Bostwick opened the door so quietly, I didn't hear her.

Chapter Two

DR. ALLAN

I NEVER EVEN HAD A CHANCE TO TELL TIM DAD WAS DEAD.
Mrs. Bostwick took charge right away, like she was in the
army, like she was the boss. First, she got the ladies to come,
"To fix 'im proper," she said. I wasn't allowed to help. I saved
that pink rose and when the ladies had Dad dressed and in
the box, I pinned it on his shirt. He'd have liked that. He
looked real dandy with it on there, even though it was a little
bit faded and limp. And Mrs. Bostwick said, "Get that thing
offa there! Have you no respeck for a dead body?" And I
said, "He's me dad and I love him true and I'm sad. But that
flower could'a made him happy, Mrs. Bostwick." And the
other ladies said, "Poor lamb, an orphan," and "'tis a hard
world for all that. If it makes an orphan girl feel better it's
the least we can do. Leave that blessed flower where it is!"

And so he looked pretty grand, really, layin' there with
his rose for all the world to see. I'd have liked to put the
proper gentleman's hat on him, too, but it's hard to wear a
hat when you're layin' down.

Mrs. Bostwick sent for the preacher and he came. Men from our building and one from the theatre came along and carried him to a cart outside. Everyone lined up on the street and took a look and then we followed the cart down the cobblestones. It seemed to make an awful loud noise, like an empty clanging. But maybe it wasn't that the cart was loud. Maybe it was that when people saw it coming they went quiet. It all happened so fast, I don't know how I felt about it all. Just kind of numb, I suppose.

Dad was buried with all the other poor people in a grave-yard far away from our street. We walked past all the big fancy stones and mossy angels looming up. The part where Dad went had small stones or wood crosses and it was by the old fence in the back corner.

It wasn't much of a ceremony. The gravediggers waited by a huge oak tree, leaning on their shovels, but they didn't have to wait long, 'cause it was a hot day and the preacher was dressed in all those black robes and he was sweating. So he said, "Ashes to ashes" and some more and then they lowered the coffin into that deep hole, and that was the end of my dad, poor Dad.

I wanted to go find Tim and just have a talk, but Mrs. Bostwick grabbed my arm and said I should go straight back to the flat. I didn't see the point; there was nobody there but me, but I went because I didn't have the energy to argue with her or run away. She can be a bit ferocious sometimes.

I walked in and lit a lamp and sat on the mattress trying to think of what to do next. But there wasn't time because Mrs. Bostwick rapped on the door and walked in, and a man was with her. He had little round spectacles, a moustache that went up, a gray frock coat with a chain across his belly and a tall silk hat, just like the one in my costume box, only cleaner. I wondered if I could nick it. He smiled at me.

"This is Gwen Peters, Doctor. She's a poor wee thing who's in need of your help. When she was only five, her mom went on to Glory. Now she's buried her poor dad just hours ago. So it's the workhouse for her, or the streets, or you. I haven't the room or the money or I'd have her meself. She hasn't any relatives that I can find out."

All this time the man was looking at me, and I was looking at Mrs. Bostwick. So this is what she meant when she said "my future"! And here she'd gone behind my back and planned out what would happen to me! She had no right! I was speechless with rage. The old cow was standing in front of the door and when I tried to slip past her she grabbed my hair and held on tight.

"She's willful, doctor, and used to getting her own way with her old dad. There'll be work to do with her, no doubt."

The man bent down in front of me and put his hand on my shoulder. "I won't hurt you," he said. "I've come because I think I can help you."

"I don't need your help," I said.

"I guess you don't," he answered, "but would you listen while I tell you about the Girls' Home?"

"If it's a story, I'll listen. If it's orders, I won't," I said.

He smiled at that and told me his name was Dr. William Allan. He'd built a bunch of "Homes" just for girls like me. He said the Girls' Home was not too far away and it had cottages where girls live together as families. He said that they go to school and to church and learn all kinds of things like sewing and cleaning, things girls need to know to go into service to gentlemen and ladies. And all the while he was talking I was making plans to run through that door, through Mrs. Bostwick's legs if I had to, and find Tim and run away forever, but then he said, "Canada."

"What?" I said.

"After the girls have been at the Home for a while and learned all there is to know, they can work in England or go out to Canada or another colony like Australia, and start a whole new life there. Would you like that, Gwen Peters?"

And suddenly I was backstage at the theatre with my dad, listening with all my heart to Pauline Johnson's words, and before I knew it, I said, "Yes!"

I gathered up my bundle and my Pauline Johnson book. I looked at my gentleman's hat for a long, long time. "I want to give this to Tim." I said. "He likes to wear it for plays, and maybe he'll still need ..." Suddenly my voice got stuck in my throat and my eyes were blurry. I looked at the mattresses on the floor, the cold stove, our table and two chairs. I looked at my old dad's sweater hanging on the hook by the door and I couldn't move.

"Dr. Allan can't be waiting around here for your friend, can he? You have to go now, Gwen," Mrs. Bostwick said. "I'll take care of all this, and make sure Tim gets the hat. You don't need to worry about another thing. You're a brave girl." She patted my shoulder. Then Dr. Allan took my hand and out we went and there was a beautiful shiny black buggy with two lovely chestnut horses just waiting for us to get in. Dr. Allan helped me up with my bundle and I left the Lane forever. Some of the neighbours and street kids had come out to wave and follow after us, but not Tim. I'd never been in a parade before and this was the second parade I'd been in that day. After we left the Lane and reached the Avenue, we clip-clopped faster. I really did feel like I was in a play. Could this be real?

The whole journey passed like that, in a sort of dream. I don't know how long we were trotting along, but the lamplighters were beginning their work just as we drove up to the Girls' Home gate. Dr. Allan got down from the buggy first and gave me his hand, like I was a real lady. We walked through the gates and went straight away into a large building and into a great hall. I counted eight other girls there, all looking as scared as me.

A woman said "Welcome" and "Behave!" and told us rules, but I couldn't listen. I was wondering where my bundle went. One minute I had it and the next minute it was gone. Before I could even ask about it, the woman bustled us outside to another building and then up a staircase. She said that Dr. Allan would be back in a moment.

There was a strange smell in the room; I wondered if there had been a fire. After a while we sat on the floor and waited. The room was big and had no furniture, only three-legged things with black boxes on top and wooden boxes nearby. Soon Dr. Allan, in shirt sleeves this time, came in and told us they were cameras. He lined us up or stood us one by one, or put us in twos and threes in front of big pictures of the streets of London, and Pop! Pop! Pop! took our pictures. We were not to smile for any of them, he said. That wasn't hard.

He told us the room was called a "stoo-dio," and said we'd done fine. He said the pictures would help him to raise money for the Homes. I couldn't think how a bunch of sad children in rags could do that, but I didn't have time to ask because another woman, Mrs. Ward, came in. She told us to follow her down the stairs and into *another* building.

Mrs. Ward got us undressed and while we stood stark naked in thin little towels, she made us stand still while she cut off all our hair. A big girl helped her. I was mad now.

"What are you cutting our hair off for?" I demanded. "No lice in *our* Homes," was all she said. The hair was piled up on the floor so deep you could almost jump in it. Some of the girls were crying, but I was too mad. The big girl swept it up and threw it in the stove. It stank.

Next they made us get into tubs of hot soapy water that smelled awful, and scrubbed half our skin off.

"Where's my bundle?" I asked when I was dry and dressed in a nightie. "It's looked after," she said. And then I saw her give the big girl a look that said, *Shhh!* so I knew they were going to take it away and keep it or burn it or something and I started to yell at her. "You can't take my costumes! You can't have my book!" I guess I was pretty loud. Mrs. Ward said there were lice in the clothes and they had to be burnt. I wanted to kick her. I worked hard to make those costumes. Dad and me had collected 138 feathers for that boa.

I ran at her and put my head down and pushed and she went "Oooof!" and was shocked but I didn't care. "Give me back my bundle!" I yelled. "Give it back!"

She grabbed my shoulders like her hands were a vice and squeezed hard and put her face up to my face. "Stop it!" she yelled. "That is *quite enough,* Missy. You will learn to obey in this place and I will personally see to it that you do. You will never, ever behave like this again. *Never."*

Her face was so close I could see the little hairs of her moustache, and the little veins on her cheeks and a bit of hair in her nose and I thought if I didn't apologize I'd have to look at that sight forever. Suddenly, I felt limp. Like all the air was out of me. I felt scared, empty and sad. I had no more energy left.

So I gave up my costumes and said in my best queen voice, "Whatever was I thinkin' of, Madame? I beg your gracious pardon." And she was so shocked that she jerked up her head, and took a deep breath. "That's better. Much better." And she told the big girl to get my book and let me keep it, so that was a comfort.

We followed Mrs. Ward into the large dining hall where we got milk and bread and jam. There were long rows of tables and chairs and windows on all sides. At the front there was a little stage and on the arch above it hung a giant photograph of our Gracious Queen, Victoria. Then a young woman named Miss Maggie stood in front of me. She was tall and wore a uniform. She had twinkly eyes and red hair. She wasn't old like Mrs. Ward. She smiled. "Gwen Peters?" I nodded.

"I'm your house mother," she said. "I'll look after you and you'll mind me when I tell you something. Come along." I followed her out of the hall, across the grass and into a little house.

Downstairs there is a playroom, a kitchen and Miss Maggie's bedroom. Upstairs there are four bedrooms. Five girls sleep in each one. The walls are blinding white. The window has a lacy white curtain. We each get our very own bed with clean sheets. My bed is against the wall by the door. The others stick out, two on one side, two on the other. Beside each bed there is a little shelf for underthings, and I've a hook for the dress and apron Maggie gave me. Maggie said that every morning we're to make our beds so tight a penny could bounce on it.

The other girls in my room were sitting up in bed, staring at me. Maggie said their names were Alice, Jean and Pet, but I was too tired to care. I was suddenly more tired than I've ever been in my life. I said hello to the girls, slipped *White Wampum* under my pillow and slept away the end of my eleventh birthday.

Chapter Three

THE GIRLS' HOME

IN THE MORNING, MAGGIE SHOOK MY SHOULDER. "COME along, Gwen Peters, wake up. It's time for prayers."

"What prayers?" I asked. "Who died now?"

"Nobody I know of. We say prayers every day in the Girls' Home. Now come on, the other girls are already downstairs. Get on your knees."

I couldn't think of what all the fuss was about and I was still tired, but I thought I'd give it a try. I got on my knees like I've seen in pictures and waited for her to start. But she didn't. She just said, "Hurry up, Gwen Peters. Just start and I'll help you if you get stuck." I folded my hands and bowed my head.

"Dear Father Christmas," I said, "This is Gwen Peters speaking."

"What?" said Maggie, a bit loud.

"I said, 'Dear Father Chris —'"

"I heard you! You're supposed to say, 'Dear Father God!' Whatever are you thinking of?"

"What's the difference?" I asked.

"Well, God is God and Father Christmas is Father Christmas!"

"But they both look the same in their pictures," I told her.

Maggie let out a little noise but I couldn't tell if it was a laugh or a sob or something else altogether. She seemed to be choking a bit. Suddenly she handed me a pair of boots and stockings, and told me to get dressed. "Hurry downstairs," she said. "We'll talk about it later."

We lined up and left the cottage and went to the dining hall and lined up again. The dining hall was full of girls sitting on benches eating porridge. We all wore the same clothes, and we all had short hair. I was reminded of the flocks of pigeons around London. But this flock was silent.

After breakfast Maggie took all the new girls up the stairs again to the stoo-dio and this time another man took our photographs. He told us to smile and look grateful and happy. I pretended I was Pauline Johnson and the crowds were going wild, so it was pretty easy.

Outside again, Maggie showed us around the Home grounds. There were other cottages and the dining hall, stoo-dio and other buildings around a big green with flower gardens and giant oak trees and even a weeping willow whose branches touched the ground. You could hide in there. Or the branches could be stage curtains for a play. On the green there was a little fountain where the sparrows and robins could come to sing and drink and bathe.

Also in the ring around the green, Maggie pointed out the school, the sewing building, the laundry building and a brand new church. I've never been a church person as Mrs. Bostwick knows, but I planned to go to this one. For one thing, there was no choice; for another they called it "The Children's Church" and I thought it was lovely to call it that. Inside I saw that they'd made the pews just the right size for a child. All the windows showed children from the Bible made up in pretty coloured glass.

Each cottage had a pretty name, like Hope, Peace, Violet, Primrose and Honeysuckle. Ours was called "Hyacinth Cottage." There were twenty girls in each house. The rule was, if you were bigger than any other girl, you must help her with her shoes and apron ties, and to obey the rules. There were a lot of rules and I didn't know if I'd ever remember them all, but since they were written out and posted in the church and dining hall and all the cottages, I guess it didn't matter, I could just read them out any time.

I could hardly believe I was there, that I was never going home again. I felt like I was in a dream. Or a play. The play would be called, "Whatever Happened to Gwen Peters?" or maybe "The Adventures of Gwen Peters." People would come for miles around to see the orphan girl who could act like anything. Of course I'd need a new boa, since mine was burnt to cinders by Mrs. Ward.

The day passed in a whirl of rules and little girls and big girls and ladies in aprons and lining up for one thing or another. Mrs. Ward showed us the sewing room and the laundry room, then quick as anything she had us in the kitchen at the back of the dining hall sitting on stools. She introduced us to Mrs. Angel, *the Lord help us if you don't mind me absolutely,* who is the matron in charge of all the food, the dining hall and the kitchen. Mrs. Angel knew everything and even told Cook what to do.

Mrs. Angel was rather fat and had a big ring of keys tied to her apron. She jingled when she walked. Her hair stuck out of her bun and even sneaked out under her mob cap, and her face was red and crinkly. She said she would teach us how to be proper maids if it was the last thing she did. She had two books on a high shelf. The fat book was called, *Mrs. Beeton's Book of Household Management* and the thin one, *The Domestic Servant*, and *the Lord help us all if they are ever touched by anyone but myself.* She said she would teach us everything we need to know about running a household. "You'll know how to lay a fire proper, and how to make plum pudding and how many potatoes to peel for dinner and how to read a recipe and make a featherbed and scour a blackened pot and ever so many other things." And then she got us peeling potatoes for dinner.

Even though I'd peeled potatoes all my life, I'd evidently been doing it wrong and leaving on too much skin or not enough skin or not digging the eyes out proper because Mrs. Angel kept coming over and putting her big fat hands on mine to show me. She kept saying, "There, there, dearie. You'll get it." And after I'd peeled about four hundred of them, I did.

By the time we'd had tea and washed dishes and prayed some more and lined up and walked here and there, it was time for bed. I slept in Room Four upstairs at Hyacinth Cottage with Jean who was twelve, Alice who was thirteen, Belle who was eight and Pet who was only four. Belle actually wasn't with us. Miss Maggie said she had the cough and went away, and so her bed was empty.

After we were in our nightdresses, we all went into the playroom and sat by the fireplace while Maggie told a story about the ladies who went on a hike. She said it all in Bible language, but the gist of the story was that Ruth, Orpah and Naomi had husbands who died and left them *bereft*. One day, Naomi said she was going home to Bethlehem, and Orpah and Ruth, who were her daughters-in-law, went with her. But Naomi said, "Go back, go back," because it was dangerous and she was sad and bitter because her husband and sons were dead. Orpah went home, but Ruth said no, she'd stay with her always. And they hiked across the wild country and got to Bethlehem. Ruth went to harvest in the fields and asked Boaz to marry her and he gave her a fifty pound sack of barley and said he would. Then she had a baby called Obed. I would *never* call my baby that, but she did. And they lived happily ever after.

That made two good stories in the Bible that you can make up plays about. Of course, if it was my story, I'd have had robbers lurking in the rocks and Ruth would have to fight them off with a huge sword she carried, and save Naomi's very life.

Then Maggie told us all to go upstairs to bed and to blow out the lamps in two minutes flat, so we did. It was very dark in our room, but after a minute I could see the outlines of the other four beds.

I put my hand under my pillow just to feel *White Wampum* before I went to sleep. It wasn't there. I got up and felt all around in the dark and under the covers and under the bed even, but it was gone. I was frantic. "My book! Where's my book?" I marched to the door to get Maggie, and Jean whispered. "Poor little sucky baby. Going to get Maggie?"

"Where's my book?"

She giggled. "What will you give me for it?" she asked.

"I'll give you a black eye if you don't give it back," I said.

Right then, Maggie called up. "What's going on up there? Girls in Room Four, settle down or you'll all be doing dishes for a week straight! Silence!"

I didn't want to tattle. I didn't want to get in trouble on my first day. But I would knock Jean's bleedin' head off if she didn't give back my book. I felt my way over to her bed and grabbed her hair. I didn't say a word, I just held on tight. She pinched me and bit my arm, but I didn't move. It seems we were like that for a long time. After a while, I pulled tighter and I heard her sob. "Stop it. That hurts." I didn't answer. Finally she said, "It's under my pillow, baby. It was just a joke."

I let go of her hair, found my book and went back to bed. "I'll get you for this, Gwen Peters," she whispered.

Chapter Four

SETTLING IN

WEEKDAYS BEGAN AT SIX-THIRTY IN THE MORNING. THAT never changed. Maggie stood at the foot of the stairs and called "Good morning, children. I expect to see you brushed, washed, dressed, lined up at the door. Prayers said, faces clean. Up now, spit spot!"

And I'd be on my feet pulling my sheets straight as a board, the gray woollen blanket tight, tight and my pillow smooth and lined up *just so* before I'd fall on my poor little knees and speak to my Maker and rhyme off the same list of God blesses as I rhymed off yesterday and the same as I'd rhyme off tomorrow and then it was run downstairs and draw a bucket of water for the other girls in the room when it was my turn and wash that face, brush that short spiky hair, grab that dress from the hook and pull it over my head, lace up my boots, tie on that apron and *hurry up* because the other girls are there already at the door, straight as soldiers. Then it was *left-right-left-right* down the steps across the green and into the dining hall.

Every day we got one bowl of porridge with cream and then cleared up the tables with the other girls on cleanup duty and got in a line and *hurry up,* over to the sewing building and *sit right down* on that stool and we'd bend our heads *quietly now* over the hemming or patching or fancy work or embroidery or whatever it was that Miss Forgrave had for us and make those damn stitches perfect or she'd make us pick them out again and picking is the most boring work God ever invented. And *not a peep out of you, Miss Peters, or you'll be picking stitches all night with no dinner break at all, do you understand me?*

If it was a bit of mending we had to do, we'd do it with joy in our little hearts because a *stitch in time saves nine* and we must always remember that little saying. It will stand us *in good stead in later years, understand?*

When the clock struck ten in the church steeple it was into another lineup so we'd hurry up and *march smartly girls,* down the steps and over to the kitchen and see what old Mrs. Angel had laid out on the long scrubbed tables to teach us about this day, *Lord help us.* Maybe to knead the biscuit dough or maybe peel about two thousand carrots. "Peel away from your clean white aprons, girls, away." The Lord help us if any of those two thousand carrots had any skin left on, or if they were peeled too thick, or somebody left on a couple of the root hairs at the bottom, because *who wants to get a root hair stuck between their teeth?* Or maybe we get a lesson on how to clean the lamp chimneys and the importance of setting a ladies table proper because it wouldn't do, Lord help us, really, it wouldn't *do* if we brought *shame to the Girls' Home* or to *Dr. Allan hisself.*

After that, it was time to do some scrubbing in the scullery or polish up that chrome on the front of the ovens so that "it shines like the sun, girls, not a streak left, not a bit of polish left, not a finger print left on it to shame the Home" and the Lord help us all if we don't do it proper because *cleanliness is next to Godliness and don't you ever forget it.*

When the clock struck noon we'd wash our hands and straighten ourselves because we've got all crooked with the cleaning and all, then line up straight and march *one-two one-two* over to the dining hall and sit down for the tea and soup that might have a bit of meat in it but might not and then clean up that dining room and wipe down those tables and straighten those benches and no laughing, there's no time for nonsense, and then march over to the school building and sit down and *open up your minds girls.*

With our minds and eyes ever so wide open it could give you a headache, we'd watch Miss Mason write on the blackboard. The chalk screeched and scratched the words up and down until we could scream, but she'd just keep on going. "Copy those words on your slates, girls. Hurry, now!" Then it was time to take turns reading a story from the Bible. One time it was about Abraham and Isaac and the Sacrifice.

"Never forget, girls, to open your minds to the story, and remember we must be willing to make the sacrifice like Abraham the loving father." She was looking over her spectacles now. "And no talking about it between yourselves. I warned you before, it's not good for you to question any of this because the story is from the Holy Bible, girls, and you have no business saying that it's not bleedin' likely that you'd let your dad truss you up with your hands and legs like that picture there, and toss you on a pile of lumber ready for the match. And you *must not say* that your old dad would never dream of doing that to you, and that's why I have to *smack you, smack you* like this on your hands with the ruler. You'll just have to learn and when you do, life will be easier for both of us, and now sit down again while I see if you know how to add up ten blackbirds and six blackbirds and four blackbirds and two more for good measure."

When the clock struck four we'd stand in line again at the door and march down the steps and out into the fresh air where we could *breathe, girls, breathe* and see the lovely green of the trees and grass and imagine being free like one of those blackbirds. But only until four-thirty because then it was time to set the tables for dinner and "you better have the forks on the left side this time, the *left side,* and lined up *just so* and not all slanted like the last time" when, Lord help us, we'd have to do it all over again.

In the dining hall there was a little framed cross-stitch picture. It read, "The devil finds work for idle hands." Well, the Lord help us all, the devil wouldn't have much to do around here.

*

One morning I realized with a shock that exactly one whole month had passed since the day I turned eleven and watched poor old Dad die. I felt like a thundering big horse had knocked me down. I could hardly get my breath. I don't know how I scrubbed the tables clean as a whistle in the dining hall, but after that I slipped out of the lineup, sneaked away and crawled through the drooping branches of the weeping willow into the green quiet.

I tried to remember Pauline Johnson's lovely voice, but it only reminded me of holding Dad's warm hand and then I started to cry and I couldn't stop. I put my arms around that willow trunk and held on tight and cried and cried. The bark felt strong and cool on my hot face, and I was glad. I missed old Dad. I missed him bringing home boa feathers from the theatre. I missed wondering if the tea is going to taste like anything at all. I missed Dad snoring me awake in the morning.

Maybe I fell asleep, I don't know, but suddenly I felt a small warm hand on my shoulder.

"Gwennie?"

It was a little voice. I turned around and it was Pet, who lives in Hyacinth Cottage with me. She was about as tall as I was, sitting down. "You sad, Gwennie?" she asked. "You wanna play?"

I blew my nose on the hankie that Maggie makes us carry in our apron pockets. "I think I have to go somewhere, Pet," I said. I peeked out at the clock in the church steeple. "I think I'm supposed to be in sewing."

"You got red marks on your face from the tree," she said. She touched my cheek tenderly with her fingers, tracing the marks, and then sat on my lap. We sat like that for a long, quiet while and rocked gently back and forth.

Pet was only four years old. Her real name was Petula, but nobody called her that.

Yesterday I had walked into our room at Hyacinth Cottage and Pet was sitting with Alice on her bed. Their backs were to me; they didn't know I was there. Alice was the one I'd hear crying herself to sleep at night.

"So you see, Pet," Alice was saying, "maybe if we're very good and do everything the way Mrs. Ward wants, we won't have to go into service. Maybe we could be adopted."

"A doctor?" asked Pet. "You want me to be a doctor, Alice?"

"Not a doctor. A-*dopted*. Like you get a new mommy and daddy to live with."

"Oh! I want to be 'dopted. That would be nice. I had a mummy once." She climbed onto Alice's lap. "Talk about 'dopted now."

Alice put her arm around Pet. "Once upon a time, I had parents. And then I didn't have them no more, so my auntie adopted me, sort of. She was splendid and funny and made up songs and never made me go to bed ..."

"And then what, Alice?"

"And then we couldn't pay the rent man and she went to the workhouse," Alice finished in a voice that was sad and soft. "And I got to come here where there's no rats."

Suddenly Jean pushed in from behind me.

"What bleedin' nonsense are you feeding the kid now?" she demanded. "You talk and talk about adoption, Alice, but it won't happen. Nobody wants us. And I'll tell you another thing. I don't want no bleedin' new parents neither. What you want parents for? To beat you up?" She looked at me. "What you staring at, sissy pants?"

"They aren't all like that, Jean," I said. "Some parents are nice —"

"Yeah. And I'm the Queen of England." I left the room then.

Now Pet looked up at me. The sun peeked through the willow leaves and made pretty shadows dance across her cheeks and forehead.

Suddenly she asked, "Can I come with you in sewing? Can I sew up a pretty dress with you like I did when my mummy was alive?"

I hugged her and laid my cheek on her head. "Let's go and see," I said. We held hands and walked across the green grass to the sewing building. About twenty girls were there on stools, sewing. When we came in they stopped and looked up.

She wasn't allowed to stay, of course. The sewing teacher was Miss Forgrave. She was tall and skinny and looked like a grasshopper. She hopped straight over and asked what was the *meaning of all this*. "You're late," she said.

"I was feeling sad," I said. "Pet helped me feel better." Miss Forgrave stared at me through her spectacles. Her mouth went in and out for a minute while she thought about that. And then she said, "The child should be in the nursery with the others. There are rules here, Missy, and you will obey them no matter how you feel! You march her right down to the nursery."

I hung my head as if I was sorry, which I wasn't, and gave Pet's hand a little squeeze. I told Miss Forgrave I didn't quite know where the nursery was and so she told Jean to do it. Jean smirked, and passed me with her nose in the air. "Yes, Miss Forgrave," she said, "Right away, Miss Forgrave."

Grasshopper gave me a towel for drying dishes and told me to hem it up quick and make sure the stitches were tiny and neat, so I did. It's not as much fun to hem towels as it is to make fairy costumes, though. I hemmed until the clock struck ten and then lined up with the others. I had to stand behind Jean.

"Ha, ha, Miss Goody Two-Shoes," she hissed. "Think you're so smart." I stuck out my tongue at her, but Miss Forgrave saw and I had to go to the back of the line. "I can see that you're a troublemaker, Gwen Peters. Once more, and I'll take you to Matron."

In the afternoon we had lessons with Miss Mason whose hair was pulled back so tight it made her eyes narrow. She rang her little bell for silence, and launched straight into a poem called "The Wreck of the Hesperus," by Mr. Longfellow. And so we sat with the captain and his *fairy-flax-eyed daughter*, while a hurricane lashed the white and fleecy waves with a *stinging blast* and everybody died. It's a tragical poem, and a good one, but the teacher was no Pauline Johnson. Instead of lifting the words off the page, she just sat there and read it so the words fell down flat on the floor.

So while Miss Mason droned her own ideas about the Wreck, I thought about how I would read it on stage and how Tim could be on the side crashing pots and pans to make thunder for the storm. Then I conjured up all the poems I could remember in *White Wampum*. And after that, I looked out the window and thought about the stories Dad used to tell me ... *Once upon a time there was a poor man who loved a princess and a prince who loved a poor girl and nobody was very happy because that sort of thing just isn't allowed ...*

That's why I wasn't paying attention when Miss Mason asked me to stand up and read the next piece, which was the story of Joseph. She had to ask twice so I got a smack on my hand with a ruler. But the story was grand.

It was about a boy who had a splendid coat with many colours. He also had wicked brothers, maybe like Jean, who sold him into slavery and he ended up in jail in Egypt and it was terrible there, probably with rats and huge insects and everything. And hungry, he was hungry all the time.

But God gave Joseph a special talent. He could understand dreams. And when the pharaoh-king found out he could do that, he took him straight out of that jail, put him on a fancy chair and made him the prime minister of Egypt. Miss Mason said Egypt was in Africa, far away, and I didn't know if it was as far as Canada or not, but I did know I'd have liked to have a coat of many colours instead of the ones we had to wear which were plain gray wool.

That night when we got into bed I felt under my pillow. My book was gone again. I felt my way in the dark to Jean's bed and reached under her pillow. She was waiting for me and grabbed my hand.

"My book, Jean," I whispered. "What will you give me for it, *crybaby?*" she asked. I made a grab for her hair but she snatched my hand and squeezed hard. I sat on her chest and pushed down and finally she whispered, "Take it."

Chapter Five

WINTER

BEFORE AUTUMN GAVE UP AND WINTER CAME, THERE WERE two sailings. About twenty children made the list to sail to Canada each time. None of the girls who went were from Hyacinth Cottage, so I didn't know them well, but the thrill of adventure rippled through us all. The night before each group left we had a celebration in the dining hall and sang special goodbye songs just for them. Most of them cried and said they would miss us all. Mrs. Ward and Dr. Allan made speeches about how Canada would welcome them and how they all made us feel proud. I envied them.

But mostly, the days were the same, just colder with each passing week. We were awake at six-thirty, prayers, breakfast, cleanup, sewing with the grasshopper, cooking with Mrs. Angel, dinner, reading and writing and tea and more cleanup and finally, bed at nine. The only surprises were the mean little tricks that Jean played on me from time to time. Her favourite was to hide *White Wampum.* Or pull my blankets crooked so I'd get in trouble with Miss Maggie for having a messy bed. Jean was like a flea bite that wouldn't heal.

On Saturdays we cleaned our cottages, scrubbed the floors, changed the sheets and took them with the dirty clothes to the laundry building for Monday wash. On Sundays we went to chapel and sang like anything and even though we were supposed to think God thoughts, sometimes I pretended I was on the stage, singing for all the world to see. It was fun as long as Matron didn't see me smiling for the audience. Then she'd pull me out of the line at the end of the service and tell me that church was *serious business* and I was to *listen* to the preacher and to think about how *thankful* I am and just whatever was I *thinking* of in there to be smiling?

One day I asked her why anyone would ever want to listen to Jesus if he never laughed or smiled. "And if he *was* jolly, why did all his pictures make him look sad?" But she brought that big face of hers up close to mine and pulled my ear nearly right off my head and said I was being *disrespectful.*

Most of all I liked looking at the stained glass windows in the church, imagining what those children were thinking about when they were sitting and having a chat with Jesus, or listening to one of his stories. I wondered sometimes if he told stories as good as my dad's. The children in the windows looked like they were listening with all their heart to what's going to happen next. I'd wonder if my dad and Jesus were floating around in the sky telling stories to all the angel children. I hoped so.

Some days, like one Saturday, we'd get a new girl. A new girl meant a new story. Over time, I'd heard a few. Pet and I were orphans. Alice was taken away from her auntie because there was no money for food. Belle's parents had to go to jail and she had to live on the street. That Saturday night just before bedtime, Maggie came in with a new girl. She said, "This is Amy. I know the girls in Room Four will make her feel welcome." I wondered what story Amy had to tell.

She looked like a scared rabbit standing there with her hair all freshly cut and her nightdress practically hanging off her skinny body. Her eyes were huge as she stood shivering, looking at us and not saying a word. I took her hand and said, "I'll look after her, Maggie." And I took her upstairs and showed her Belle's bed. Belle won't be coming back.

I told Amy all about the rules and the praying, to watch out for Grasshopper, to mind Mrs. Ward and not to let her see if she was having any fun at all. When Jean came in, she looked at Amy and Amy looked at her. "So they got you, too," is what she said. Amy didn't answer.

Pet came in and sat close beside her and when she put her little hand on Amy's rough, chapped one, Amy stared at Pet and then at the hands on her lap like she'd never seen anything like them in her life. Then she gave a great big yawn. So we let her be and went downstairs for a story. When we came back, Amy was fast asleep.

Amy was eleven like me. She didn't talk much the first day. But then I remembered what I'd felt like when I first got here. It was sort of a shock. By the second day, I'd made her laugh. After school on the third day I told her all about *White Wampum* and Miss Pauline Johnson from Canada and how I was going to be an actor, *don't tell Matron,* and all about Tim and about going to Canada some day, and about my poor old dad.

The next day, she talked. She told me about living in the same building as Jean when they were small, and how they played together in the gutters. She told how her mom used to get mean drunk something awful, and how they were hungry all the time. She said that Jeannie, that's what she calls Jean, had big bruises on her arms and legs all the time because her parents beat her and beat her and beat her all the time.

One day, when Jean's eye was smacked so hard it was swollen shut, they both ran away from home. They lived with an old woman who made them sell matches on the street to pay for being lodgers in the woman's house.

"There was rats as big as dogs," Amy said. "And so many people sleeping in that room you could hardly move your arms to shoo them away. It stank something awful, and at night all you could hear was snoring and coughing and people talking in their sleep or crying ..."

I didn't say a word. I just sat there watching as her eyes looked away, remembering that room. "I was used to fleas in me bed, Gwen," she said, "but these was worse. These fleas hopped off dirty old men and horrible old hags ..." Her voice trailed off as she scratched her leg where memory gave her an itch. "What happened next?" I asked.

"We lasted three or four weeks there, I guess. Then we shoved off and learned to live on the streets. Sometimes it was fun, but mostly it was cold and I was hungry all the time."

"Didn't you nick what you needed in the markets?" I asked. "My friend Tim is good at that."

"Don't be daft, Gwen Peters," she said. "Of course we

did. You didn't want me starving to my death, did you? One night, we were sleeping behind a greengrocer's and four men sneaked along the alley and found us. Suddenly, they raised up their lanterns and near blinded us with light. They grabbed Jean and three of the boys and took them away, quick, like that!" She snapped her fingers. "They didn't see me. I was in the shadows under a pile of cabbage leaves. I was scared. I could hear Jean screaming and cussing for a long time when they drove away, clip-clop, down the street. I thought maybe she was in the workhouse, or jail. I never knew she'd ended up here. Funny how the same thing's happened to me now."

"But what happened to you next?"

Amy looked out the window. "I lived on the street with the other kids. We looked after each other out there."

I thought of Tim again.

"And then the men came again. This time they caught me."

"I'm glad you're here, Amy."

She smiled. "It's better than the workhouse, isn't it?"

"Yes," I said. "Jean, though, she doesn't like me one bit."

"Don't pay her no never mind. She's always been like that. The secret is, don't let it bother you and then she'll come around. You'll see."

I thought for a long time about Jean. I kept trying to imagine why anyone would beat up a little girl only as big as Pet, only I couldn't. I read in a book once about a woman "whose heart swelled with love," and I didn't know what it meant, but when I thought about Jean as a little girl, I have to admit that my heart did something strange.

After Amy had settled in a bit, Jean seemed less angry and

her mean tricks slowly stopped. The next time my book went missing I didn't say a word. The following night it was under my pillow again.

The next week it was so cold you had to wear a bonnet and coat just to go to the sewing room or the laundry or anywhere. One day we were in the dining hall finishing our tea. Suddenly Mrs. Ward banged a spoon on the table and said, "Attention, girls!"

We all put down our spoons and sat up straight to listen.

"I have a special announcement. Do you all know what's coming up soon?"

"No, Mrs. Ward," we said in a chorus.

"It's Christmas, girls."

"Yes, Mrs. Ward," we answered in one voice.

"And what does Christmas mean here in the Girls' Home, girls?"

I looked around the table at the other girls and tried to imagine what she meant. Did Father Christmas come here?

No one answered, because no one knew.

"It means that we'll have a concert! And who will come to the concert, girls?"

Again, no one answered. I just wished she'd tell us instead of talking like we were all daft.

"Dr. Allan, the Father of 'Nobody's Children,' that's who!" she cried. She was excited, you could tell. I had been hoping for a different father, but Dr. Allan would have to do. He was kind enough when he came to our flat and brought me here. It seemed that day was about a hundred years ago, instead of six months.

So, the next three weeks, besides all our regular routine, and besides making gifts for the girls and Maggie, we made paper snowflakes and stars to decorate the dining hall. We also had choir practice and drill practice and learned some recitations for the concert, and I had many suggestions for how to make the pageant better. Like, I could tell about how the angels got there, flying through the dark night over the rooftops of London and all that, but Maggie said, "No, we'll just keep to the Bible," and after a few more suggestions for making the performances really good, I gave up and let her do it her way. Anyway, I knew Mrs. Ward would kill us if we did anything too different. It's a good story, so I just let it be.

Three days before the concert Mrs. Ward herself came to get me out of sewing class. Trailing after her to the administration building I tried to imagine what I'd done wrong. When I went in, I got a big shock. Tim and Mrs. Bostwick were standing there, with melting snow starting to make a puddle on the floor. What a Christmas gift! Mrs. Bostwick swept me to her bosom and I near suffocated with the smell of violets, but oh, it was so good to be hugged. Tim's feet were poking out of his shoes. He must have been frozen, but he smiled at me like he was made out of sunshine.

Mrs. Ward went away and the three of us sat down. "Jest look at yerself!" Mrs. Bostwick said over and over again. When Mrs. Ward returned with tea in real tea cups, Tim said, "Thanks for your letters, Gwen. Your writing is very good. You must have had a good teacher."

I was about to tell him all about Miss Mason and then I saw his smile. He meant his own self! I laughed. "I had the best," I said. "And you could write to me, too, Tim. Mrs. Bostwick will give you paper and stamps, I'm sure."

"Won't need charity soon, Gwen. I'm getting a real job soon enough. I'm going to be delivering newspapers. You'll see."

I wanted to ask if Mrs. Bostwick had given him the hat and if he still had it, but I felt shy to ask that when here he was talking about going off to be a working man.

Mrs. Bostwick gave me the news from the Lane and hugged me again, wishing me a grand Merry Christmas. By the time all the snow had melted off their boots and hats into puddles on the floor, it was time for them to go.

The day before the concert, boys from the Boys' Home brought in the most beautiful, best-smelling fir tree in the world and set it up right in the dining hall. It was the first time I'd ever had a tree. I touched its branches. They were prickly but soft. The green smell stayed on my finger tips for a long time after I left the room. The big girls decorated it with a tin star on the top and paper chains that the little girls had made and little paper angels. It was very beautiful.

On Christmas Eve we went to church and prayed to *Almighty God* and said thanks to God for sending baby Jesus. We sang "Joy to the World" and I wondered, with all the hundreds of us singing our little hearts out and filling up that whole high church with music, if the heavenly angels could hear us. And what was it *like* for Mary to lay her child in a lowly manger, anyway?

After that we said a lot of *begottens* and *manifesteds* and *hereins*, and we blessed all the *less fortunate people* and prayed for *peace on earth* and then we blessed all the whole wide world. It was hard to sit still through the rest; we could hardly wait to get to the dining hall for the concert.

All the tables had been pushed to the sides and the benches were in rows facing the end that was our stage. Mrs. Allan, holding a baby, and Dr. Allan, holding his tall silk hat like Tim's, came in and sat at the front. For a moment I felt a terrible pain in my stomach because I missed being around Tim like anything, and I even said a little prayer for God to give Tim a good Christmas like me and some shoes without holes in them for the winter.

Mrs. Ward called up the choir and we sang "Away in a Manger" and I saw Dr. Allan and Mrs. Allan wipe away a few tears, so we must have been good.

All the girls who were eleven like me performed an "evergreen drill," which means we all had little branches of fir and we marched around in formation in two lines that crisscrossed in the middle and made patterns while Mrs. Angel played a marching tune on the piano. When we heard one special note it meant "hold up your branch" and another note meant, "swing it from left to right in time with the music." At the end, we all got to line up in a row and curtsey and everyone clapped like we were marvelous.

The last part of the concert was the pageant that tells the Christmas story. We even had costumes for this, so I loved this best of all. Pet and I got to be angels. Amy got to be Mary, and I was glad. There were about twenty-five of us in it, counting the shepherds. We had a doll for Jesus. We were almost ready to start when Pet darted over to Mrs. Allan and asked in a loud whisper, "Could the baby be Jesus?" Mrs.

Allan leaned down and said, "No, dear, this baby is a girl." And then she looked at Pet's sad face and said, "Why not?" Pet ran to the manger and took out the doll and Mrs. Allan put the sleeping baby in and then we started.

Maggie read the story out of the Bible about Mary and Joseph going to Bethlehem and there was no room at the inn for them, so poor old Joseph had to take Mary into the barn to have her baby Jesus there with all the cows and sheep and cobwebs and all that, and then Lo! the shepherds watching their flocks on the hills around got a visit from the heavenly hosts and that's where we came in. Heavenly hosts are angels.

Pet and I were both angels, but Pet had the line. I helped her practise her words like anything. She had to say, "Behold! I bring you tidings of great joy!" But Pet didn't know what it meant, so how could she say it right? I told her that it meant, "Hello! I've got some good news!" and then she knew. But sometimes, she got it confused. "Behold! I've got good tidings!" and we'd have to start again. She had to remember the line and she had to almost yell it since there would be a lot of people at the concert and the people at the back had to hear.

On we went, wrapped in white sheets and wire wings. "Behold!" Pet said loudly, "I bring you tidings of great joy." Then she did a little twirl and yelled, "It's a girl!" Then the angel choir sang, "Silent Night, Holy Night!" and the shepherds knew what they had to do next, which was go to see that new baby. No one ever mentioned Pet's extra words, and neither did she.

After the concert Dr. Allan made a little speech. He said how proud he was of us. He said how we had blossomed into flowers, the best flowers.

"Your safety and the promise of a good life are my reward," he said. "By your obedience, cheerfulness and hard work, you pay me for my work on your behalf. Be good little girls! And have a Merry and Blessed Christmas!" And after that we all lined up and he went down the line with Mrs. Allan and they gave each of us an orange and a little piece of cardboard with the Lord's Prayer written on it and a picture of Jesus. It's quite a good likeness, I think. I've never had an orange before. It was juicy and round and it smelled grand. I ate half of it right away and saved the rest for Christmas Day.

In the morning Pet bounced on my bed and said, "Behold, Gwennie! It's Christmas!" and she gave me a white stone, and on it was a gray mark, almost like it was made by hand, but it wasn't. It looked like the outline of a star. "That's to remember being angels," she said. I told her I loved it and would keep it forever. *Forever*.

We all got dressed and went downstairs and Maggie already had the lamps lit and the fire stoked. She had made each of us a handkerchief with our initial embroidered in the corner. I gave Pet a doll I made out of scraps from the sewing room and she named her Lucy-Gwen. I gave Maggie pressed flowers tied with a piece of red ribbon and she liked that. For Jean and Amy, I had copied out "The Song My Paddle Sings" from *White Wampum*. I used my best handwriting and drew pictures of how I remember Miss Pauline Johnson when I saw her perform in her blue silk dress. Amy hugged me. Jean started to cry and ran upstairs. When I went up after her she was lying on her bed.

"Don't you like the poem?" I asked. But she was crying

too much to answer at first, so I just stood and waited.

"I don't have a gift for you," she said. I told her that was alright.

"Why did you give me a gift when I've been mean to you and called you a baby?"

"I don't know," I said. "I guess because you're sad." And I waited some more to see what would happen.

"I'm sorry I was mean," she said. "Do you think we could be friends?"

"Alright," I said. "Let's go downstairs." And we did.

We didn't have to go to school or into sewing or laundry and we even had roast goose and Christmas pudding for a feast and altogether, it was a grand Christmas Day.

That night, when everyone was sleeping, I wrapped my quilt around me and tiptoed to the window. The village was dark; nothing moved. The crescent moon hung low in the clear, starry sky. I wondered which of the stars was Dad. "I miss you," I whispered to the window, "I'll be going into 1896 without you."

And suddenly I remembered last New Year's when I had to help him home from the pub and half carry him up the stairs. He was singing.

I remember that lassie, the fair lady Gert,
Bless me, my son, but that woman could flirt,
She'd flutter her lashes, she'd raise up her skirt,
O how I do miss her, the fair lady Gert.

I was trying to shush him, when all at once Mrs. Bostwick stormed into the hall in her nightdress and cap.

"What's the meaning of this, you disgraceful man!" she roared, "You're drunk!"

"Why, Gwennie!" Dad said. "Look who's here! It's our kindly neighbour, out for a stroll in the park, she is! It's a very fine outfit you're wearing, Mrs. B., all trussed up like a fat Christmas goose and ready for the oven!"

Mrs. Bostwick turned beet red. "Humph!" she said. "And in front of the child, too. Shame on you! Get into bed quick, before I call the coppers on you!" And she slammed her door so hard I thought it would snap clean off the hinges. We both fell down laughing 'til we had tears running down our faces! Remember?

I wish you were here, Dad.

Chapter Six

VISITORS

EACH MORNING THAT WE WALKED ACROSS THE GREEN I SAW more flower buds bursting open. Spring had come in a rush of colour and beautiful fragrances. One morning, Pet crawled into bed with me and said, "Happy Birfday, Gwennie!" Her warm little body snuggled under the covers. I made puppets out of my stockings and we put on a Punch and Judy show for Jean, Amy and Alice. We had fun until, "Good morning, children. Let me see you brushed, washed, dressed, lined up at the door. Prayers said, faces clean. Up now, spit spot!" And that was the end of that.

After prayers and porridge in the dining room, Amy picked some forget-me-nots from the garden and gave them to me to press in a book so I would always remember her. If Mrs. Ward had seen her do that, she'd be in big trouble, but she hadn't been caught, and it was all the more lovely that her gift was a secret and a little bit dangerous.

Jean and Alice wrote a poem for me and said it together. It was called "Good Friends" and I told them I would treasure it forever. I put it in my book with the forget-me-nots. Pet gave me a black stone from the garden, round and smooth. "It's magic, Gwennie," she told me. "If you hold it and make a wish, the angel fairies will make it happen." I told her I would look after it and keep it with my special Christmas stone forever.

I can hardly believe I've been here a whole year. I thought about poor old Dad for a while and wondered if he was floating with the angels and if he was with Mum and if they were looking at me from the clouds. I hoped so. I hoped they knew that things had worked out alright for me.

It was lunch time when Mrs. Ward herself came to get me. "You have visitors," she said. "Come along." And I did, with all the girls at the table staring and staring after me.

It was Mrs. Bostwick and Tim again! I was so happy to see them I began to cry and Mrs. Bostwick said, "There, there, what's all this, then?" and she pulled out a handkerchief and wiped my eyes and then her own. Tim went from one foot to the other and didn't say much, but I could tell he was glad to see me. He's grown. He's much taller than me now, but then, he's two years older.

"Tim wouldn't hear of me coming without him," Mrs. Bostwick said. "He's been worrying me since Christmas about coming over again."

Mrs. Ward looked at Tim's raggedy shirt with only two buttons and his raggedy hair sticking out at the back and said it was quite alright and that it was nice for a girl to have callers especially on her birthday, and *please won't you sit down?* And then she sent a big girl to fetch some tea in real tea cups for us all.

Mrs. Bostwick told me all the news from the Lane, who had died and who'd had a baby and who lived in our old flat. She eyed me up and down like I was a prize chicken at the butcher's and said she thanked *God Almighty* that she'd thought of sending me here and *My, haven't you filled out even since Christmas, Gwen.* Then she turned all her attention to Mrs. Ward, so I finally got a chance to ask Tim how he was. Did he still go to the Ragged School and read books?

"I don't have time for that no more," he said. "I'm working now." And he looked at me sharp so I'd be impressed and I was.

"I'm selling newspapers, Gwen. I got the job. I've made quite a few bob, too." And then he lowered his voice and said he was saving his money and he was going to go to the colonies and start a farm and there was any number of ships sailing out of England and the land could be had for free and he was going to be a gentleman farmer with acres and acres of land. It was only a matter of time. But first he thought he'd go to Africa.

"Africa? What for?"

"There's gold there, Gwen," he said. "You can pick it up off the ground."

"Go on!" I said in disbelief. "That's a good story."

"No. It's true. I read it in the newspaper. There's gold in Africa and in Canada. And jewels in India. Why, the whole British Empire is full of riches! There's lots of money out there, if a man goes to get it."

I thought about that for a minute.

"I could get rich, Gwen. I could buy a whole theatre, never mind just perform in one. And buy a farm, or anything at all! And when I do, I'll come back and get you." ·

I didn't know what to say.

"It sounds grand, Tim. Just grand." And then I blurted it out. "I've been thinking of going to Canada myself," I said. "To see where Miss Pauline Johnson lives and to be an actor and all. Dr. Allan will send me if I work hard."

"Can Dr. Allan really get you to Canada?" he asked.

"Some of the girls I met here last year have already sailed. You take a train from London, then sail from Liverpool."

"So I guess that's it, then. When? When are you going?"

Suddenly, Mrs. Bostwick clapped her tea cup down in the saucer and said, "My, my, look at the time, Tim!"

I felt desperate to make the visit last longer. To make Tim stay. To not let him go to Africa or wherever he was going. I felt scared all of a sudden. "Tim?"

He was looking at the floor, at the ceiling, at the walls, but not at me. "Tim?" He blinked a few times. "Write to me."

"We must be off!" Mrs. Bostwick said loudly. With her skirts swishing and Tim trailing behind in his too-short pants, they were gone. I waved until they were out the gate and then I stood there, alone. Mrs. Ward said, "Well, then, that's over. Come along, no mooning. Into the dining room for clearing up." I felt very lonely.

The next morning I woke up with blood in my bed and on my nightdress and I couldn't think what was wrong. I didn't hurt, but I was obviously bleeding to death. I was dying, without ever seeing Canada or finding out if Tim got rich in the colonies, or performing on a real stage!

When Pet came to snuggle into bed with me, I had to tell her to go away. I felt bad, but how could I let her into my death bed? How could I even explain? And it was even more tragic that I sent her away from me, crying. I knew that I'd have to lie there. Forever. That I had to lie there and slowly let my life leave me, while Pet wailed and sobbed downstairs. I folded my hands like you do when you're dead and closed my eyes and waited for the end. I hoped someone would pin a rose on me for my burial.

Amy, Jean and Alice told me to hurry up and rushed out to line up at the door. Miss Maggie called me, but I didn't answer. What could I say?

Maggie, I knew, would be sad when I finished dying, because she liked me and was glad when I helped with Pet and tried to be good. And I know she liked my stories and plays and poems. And as I thought about how much she would miss me, the tears sneaked out from under my eyelids and rolled slowly into my ears. I didn't brush them away; I just waited.

Maggie's voice came into my ears, too. "Spit spot, Gwen Peters! What is the meaning of this? Are you ill?" I didn't open my eyes. I just said, "I'm dying, Maggie. Farewell."

"Open your eyes! Tell me what is wrong! Shall I get Mrs. Ward?"

"It won't make any difference, Maggie. Just tell her good-bye for me."

There was a silence, and then suddenly she whispered, "You wouldn't happen to be bleeding to death, would you?"

I sat up. "How did you know?" I asked.

Maggie sent the others out to breakfast and sat on the edge of my bed. She took a deep breath and then explained the wonder of being a woman to me. She said that the bleeding was a perfect miracle of nature and how it meant that one day I'd be able to have children of my own. She explained how I was to cut strips of cotton cloth to catch the blood and not to worry at all, at all. She said this would happen every month now until I was very old and that she has it, and every woman in the world has it, and that it's God's plan and so it must be a holy thing. I was not dying; I was instead, a woman!

Maggie helped me with the cloths and pulled the sheets off and got fresh ones for me and we made the bed and I kept thinking, "I've got a miracle inside me!" the whole time, and I couldn't stop smiling.

When I went into the dining hall, I looked at Amy and Jean and Alice and they smiled little tiny smiles, secret smiles. And then I knew that they knew. It was like I'd entered a secret club of girls ... no ... young *ladies*. I liked it.

Chapter Seven

ROYAL PERFORMANCE

IT WAS ON THE TWENTY-FOURTH OF MAY, OUR DEAR QUEEN Victoria's birthday, that we next saw Dr. Allan. We had pushed back all the tables and added more chairs in the dining room, so that the hundreds of us could all get in together, like at Christmas. The older girls had hung up Union Jack flags and added more pictures of Queen Victoria herself. They'd put flowers at the front of the hall and hung up splendid red, white and blue bunting. They had also hung up the biggest map of the world you can imagine. All the British Empire was coloured pink. We learned all about that in school. It really was like a birthday party for a queen. Only she wasn't there, of course. She was probably over at the palace opening up a thousand presents and eating cake in her diamonds and crown and all that.

After all the girls were seated, Mrs. Ward led in Mrs. Allan with her swishing gray silk dress and Dr. Allan all dressed up with his tall silk hat, frock coat and gold watch. They sat on a platform right under a big picture of Queen Victoria's head.

When Mrs. Angel went to the piano, we all stood up straight as pokers and sang:

God save our gracious Queen,
Long live our noble Queen,
God save our Queen.
Send her victorious,
Happy and glorious,
Long to reign over us,
God save the Queen.

I know that Allan girls have been saved from the workhouse. I'm not exactly sure what God is supposed to have saved the Queen from, but it's a good song anyway. Then Mrs. Ward said a prayer for the Queen's health and asked God to bless the whole wide world, especially the part that was British.

Then she said, "Long live the Queen!" and we all said, "Long live the Queen!" back to her and sat down. Next, Mrs. Ward made a whole speech about *our gracious Queen* who has reigned over us kindly for fifty-nine whole years. I can't imagine being as old as that.

She said that we were all proud to be part of the glorious British Empire, *on which, girls, the sun never sets.* She added in how *grateful* we are to live in the Girls' Home, and how *grateful* we are to Dr. Allan who works so *tirelessly* for the good of the *poor, unfortunate, destitute orphans, paupers, strays and waifs.* She meant us, the girls at the Home. Then Mrs. Angel struck the chords for "Jesus Loves the Little Children:"

Jesus loves the little children
All the children of the world,

Red and yellow, black and white,
They are precious in his sight,
Jesus loves the little children of the world.

It made me feel happy to sing that, and we sang it loud and Mrs. Angel played it so hard she was sweating when we'd finished all the verses.

Finally, Dr. Allan stood up and made a speech. He said he was proud of us. He told us how he had given thirty years to us, to make sure that we would have *opportunities* in life. "Jesus loves us," he said, "and I love you, too." He talked about his work in the Boys' Home, in the Ragged Schools, in the Babies' Castle in Kent and in Edinburgh Castle where he preaches to thousands of people on Sundays. He told us about his Boys' Industrial Farm in Manitoba, Canada where hundreds of boys from the London slums were farming. They make cheese and butter, grow vegetables and look after cows and pigs and they are ever so happy in all that fresh air. His moustache went up and down like a pump, he was so excited.

He told how there were *opportunities* for each of *us* in the colonies: fresh air and sunshine and plenty of food and work for people who wanted it. "Canada is a new heaven and a new earth," he said, and we'd be able to sail across *the golden bridge* and be welcomed by Canadians who now live in this new earth. He said there were places for boys on the farms and for girls as mother's helpers and servants. People in Canada were *crying* for trained young people who would help with the children, or serve as maids — not just any maids, but maids who understood all about running a house properly in the English way. He said Canada *needs* us, that

Canada would *welcome* us with open arms. "From the shores of Ontario the cry is heard, 'Come over and we will help you!'"

And we clapped and clapped when he talked because he made us feel so happy. And then he said, "And which of you would like to *go* to this golden land of opportunity? Just put up your hand and show me!"

You could have heard a flea breathe, it was so quiet in the hall. Then my hand went up so fast it almost shot off my arm. At last! Pauline Johnson and silver birch and the shining mountain and canoes. And Amy and Pet, Jean and Alice flung up their hands — all the girls in our whole row did! It was hard to stay on the seat, it was that exciting.

As if that wasn't enough, then Dr. Allan told us about the Royal Albert Hall performance and said that he wants the evergreen drill girls from the Christmas concert to be in it! And His Royal Highness, if you please, Prince Albert *himself*, will be in attendance.

Later on, we sang some more and then it was the end. Or maybe it was the beginning.

The next day, Mrs. Ward wrote my name on a long list, along with Pet and Jean and Amy and Alice. Pet is only little, so she wouldn't have to work. Some of the small ones and even babies get to be adopted into a real family.

After that, things moved quickly. All the children on the sailing list had to have a medical examination. When I was on my poor little knees saying my God Blesses the next day, I God-blessed the doctor, too. Jean, Amy, Pet, Alice and I all passed the test. We were set to leave July third from Liverpool, England. I saw where that is on the map in the schoolroom.

Next, Mrs. Ward posted a packing list in each cottage. Each girl was to get her things ready for the sailing. This meant sewing until your eyeballs nearly fell out of your head. The list had things like four pair woollen drawers, two pinafores, two petticoats, one coat, one pair sturdy boots, one hat, two handkerchiefs.

I did wonder, though, how it would feel to leave England, maybe forever. And I did wonder what it would be like living so far from Tim and even Mrs. Bostwick. I wrote each of them a long letter as soon as I had the details of our sailing. I took out two little bluebird feathers from where I kept them in my book, treasures I had found under the willow tree. I slipped one in each of the envelopes, and before I thought about it too much more, I licked the glue and sealed them. It was better to stay busy than to think too much right now. And so I did.

We were all awfully busy, what with sewing and imagining Canada and practising for the performance at the Royal Albert Hall. We were so busy, in fact, that at first no one noticed when Pet became especially quiet. But suddenly, Maggie did notice. And then we all did. Pet was much too quiet. When I felt her head, it was very hot. We took turns cooling her forehead with wet cloths and wrapped her up tight, but in the night Maggie went for Mrs. Ward. When Maggie carried her downstairs to the infirmary, Pet's face was red and her hair was wet with sweat. I slipped the black fairy stone she'd given me for my birthday into Pet's hand. I told her to hold on, hold on tight and wish for God and the angel fairies to make her well.

A week later, a horse and cart delivered fifty beautiful new trunks that were made at the Boys' Home in the carpentry shop. They even had locks on them. Everyone who would be sailing was given a trunk and on the top was painted each girls' name! It was exciting to begin packing at last! The first thing I put in was *White Wampum*. The next thing I packed was a gift from Dr. Allan. He had sent each girl a Bible of our very own. He even wrote our names inside. And in it, he placed a photograph of himself so we will remember him forever.

Before the packing was done, though, the day of the performance arrived. Three thousand Allan children performed that night, girls and boys, even children on crutches. Even the babies got to be on the stage; no one was left out. I shall never forget it. It was June 24th.

Right after breakfast we started out for Royal Albert Hall. Waiting in the queue on the sidewalk, I read all the signs pasted on the walls: "Dickens' Oliver Twist," "The Pirates of Penzance by Gilbert and Sullivan," "Mendelssohn" and "Verdi," whoever they are. Going around to the back, though, the sign that gave me a shiver was the sign on the door we went in: "Stage."

After the audience filled up all the seats, they all stood up again when the Prince and Princess of Wales came in. First we sang "God Save the Queen," and then we sang "God Bless the Prince of Wales." Then Dr. Allan walked to the middle of the stage and stood under the huge banner that read, "Welcome to their Royal Highnesses from the largest family in the world." That was us.

The first act was the boys who did a drill dressed up in work clothes to show they were going to be blacksmiths, bakers, carpenters, shoemakers, tinsmiths, tailors and cooks.

Dr. Allan said that almost half of the five thousand children in his care were girls, *little sisters in orphanhood and destitution,* and that's where I came on. My group was the ironing girls, and while the Boys' Band played, we marched across that stage and criss-crossed at the right time and the gas lights lit us up like we were regular stage queens. Irons are heavy as anything when you're ironing in the laundry building. But when you're waving it for an audience with the Prince and Princess out there, an iron is light as a feather.

We did our drill perfectly, us with our irons, others hanging out clothes, sewing, and baking. After that came the crippled children. They crawled and limped and walked on crutches and played a game of cricket. Next were the babies. They didn't do much of anything except lie in prams and playpens. And even though some of them were crying, the audience cheered.

After that Dr. Allan introduced "the flower of my flock," the ones picked to go to Canada. Our act was called, "Tested and Trained for Travel: *enroute* to the Far West." I got to be in this one, too. There were boys and girls in this one, and the girls even got to put on red hoods and carry market bags. It wasn't like wearing a Mohawk dress, or carrying a boa, but it was still good.

The stage had been set up to look like Canada on one side and England on the other. We marched onto the stage and then stopped so Dr. Allan could ask the audience for money and prayers for us since we were leaving England. He said, "May God guide and bless my dear boys and girls and bring them all safely to the haven of their dreams." Then Dr. Allan gave the signal, the boy's band began to play, and we split into two groups. Some of us went to the Canada side of the stage and the others waved at us with white handkerchiefs. I got to hold up a flag that said, "Goodbye" on it. We were marvelous! The crowd really did go wild. Oh, my dad would have been proud.

It took me ever so long to get to sleep that night. I kept going over and over it in my mind and hearing the crowds clapping and clapping for us. In the morning, I counted. There were only nine days left before we sailed for Canada. If only Pet could be with us.

Chapter Eight

GOODBYE ENGLAND

THE AFTERNOON SUN WAS BRIGHT THE LAST DAY. MRS. WARD introduced Miss Tweed whose job it was to get us safe and sound to Liverpool. Then Mrs. Ward went down our line and hugged us and wiped her eyes. Dr. Allan met us at the train station. He climbed up on a trunk and said a prayer *to God bless* us on our way across the golden bridge. The train came puffing and spitting along the track with smoke and cinders flying. The men loaded our trunks and then one by one, we climbed the step and settled into our seats. I could hardly believe I'd come here only last year. It seemed I'd always lived with *the Lord help us, left-right-left* and *faces clean, spit spot!*

It was a short ride to London. Arriving at the noisy station, full of smoke and steam, the crowds and the clamour nearly knocked me off my feet. Holding hands and sticking close behind Miss Tweed, we Home Girls kept sharp eyes about us as we walked from one train to the next, the overnighter to Liverpool. The bell clanged. The station master roared, "All aboard!" and we puffed slowly away from home. I planned to stay awake all night, to think about Tim and Dr. Allan and the girls left behind at the Home … but the stuffiness in the car and the swaying of the train rocked me to sleep soon after the lights of London disappeared. I dreamed that Pet was with us, snuggling up beside me with her sweet smile.

I woke up with a stiff neck, no Pet and an urge to use the toilet. The thought of trying to do that while the train swayed back and forth didn't appeal to me, so I decided to wait 'til we reached Liverpool. I sat up snug to the window and while the sun rose, I watched the farms, forests and villages roll past. This England was a whole new world. Children waved from the ditches. Cows and sheep grazed peacefully in the fields. Now that I've seen a real cow, I guess Mrs. Bostwick doesn't look like one after all.

After we'd eaten everything that Mrs. Angel had packed for our breakfast, we chugged slowly toward the smoke stacks, church steeples, houses and factories that make up Liverpool. Everything I'd ever known was behind me now. The adventure was ahead. *Farewell, Pet, Mrs. Bostwick, Tim, Mrs. Ward, Mrs. Angel. Farewell.*

Miss Tweed handed us over to Miss Dorgan at the station. She is in charge of us now, and will take us all the way to Canada, and make sure we don't get lost or fall off the ship and into the sea. She was dressed in black from head to toe with only a wisp of white lace at her throat. She held a black parasol over her head and poked at the air. "Follow me, girls!" she called. "Hold hands. Keep your eyes on my parasol!" And we were off into the noisy streets of Liverpool.

I'd lived inside the walls of the Home for more than a year, only leaving it once. I'd forgotten how exciting city streets can be. We struggled along to the musical calls of the vendors, "Lem-onade!" "Gin-ger beer! Only a penny!" Match sellers were waving their little boxes under our noses, flower girls and fish mongers calling out "Roses! Buy me roses!" "Fresh hot eels! Get 'em while they're hot!" I was fair out of breath with all the busyness, and we had to make ourselves small to squeeze by the fruit sellers and taffy pullers, all pushing and shoving and jostling to get attention.

As we made our way through the crowds toward the docks, my head nearly swivelled off my neck a hundred times. The smells of the sea and hot tar and food and dirt floated on the warm Liverpool breeze. Children laughed, played and cried and fought. Adults laughed and hollered at each other and told the children not to fight. There was so much to see! A little white dog chasing a great brown dog with sausages hanging out of his mouth cut through our line. On our left, little children screamed with laughter as they watched a Punch and Judy show. On our right, three women marched to and fro holding signs: "Votes for Women!" "Equal Rights for Women!" "Safe work places for Everyone!" A crowd had gathered to listen to a woman make a speech. We slowed to watch.

"We *will* have the vote," she said.

"And I'm a monkey's uncle!" sneered a man at the back of the crowd.

"Your family history has nothing to do with women having the right to vote, sir," she replied. I laughed and looked at her admiringly. She didn't look like she was afraid of anyone at all. The crowd whistled and cheered.

"Come along, girls! Don't dawdle," called Miss Dorgan.

"But who are they?" I asked.

"Fawcett's women, and nothing to do with us," Miss Dorgan snapped.

"But ..." I said, wondering who Fawcett was.

"No buts. They're just *suffragettes*. Wild women who want to *vote*, of all things. Now come along!" I looked over my shoulder as we trotted along and saw a tall man grab a woman's arm and drag her away, "Get on 'ome, woman, for the love of God!" he roared.

Liverpool church ladies met us near the dock and gave us each a jam tart and a little Union Jack flag. We were all quiet for a bit while we ate the sticky tarts, and then the ladies helped Miss Dorgan line us up and march us, all holding our little flags, to the dock to get on the row boats that took people out to the ships.

Suddenly, everything seemed to stop. The sights, smells and sounds of Liverpool around me faded and disappeared. All I could see was the great, throbbing water and the teeny, tiny boats that would carry us to the ship.

But there was no time to think about my thumping heart or the bobbing boats or the jam tart that slipped out of my stomach and climbed back up into my throat due to the fact that I couldn't swim and there were likely whales just under the water waiting to swallow us up like Jonah, because Miss Dorgan stirred the air with her black parasol. "Hurry along, girls!" she called, as if there was nothing terrifying about any of this. I hoped she was right.

Then it was *step lively, girls* into the boats and *climb smartly, girls* onto the ship and *walk briskly, girls,* along the deck and down into our cabins.

Our trunks were already magically down there. I got a top bunk and hoped I wouldn't knock my brains out on the ceiling because there wasn't much room between it and me.

It was a bit dark down there, but cozy. The ship didn't bounce around like the little boats had. Maybe it would be alright. I shared the cabin with Alice, Amy and Jean and three other Home Girls who were older than us and didn't talk to us. There wasn't a lot of room with our trunks and all of us, but it didn't matter because I planned to go on deck and watch the sea. I just wouldn't stand close to the railing, that's all. After we made sure the trunks we had were our own, we were allowed to go on deck and watch the men loading the hold.

Finally, the ship's whistle blasted three times. On the docks a little band played "There'll Always Be an England." The music drifted ragged across the water. People waved from shore. Some of the girls cheered and waved, but I had a lump in my throat and so I just stood there as the dock got smaller and smaller in the distance. I watched the sun lighting up England until England was just a speck of land in the vast, gray sea.

Alice, Amy, Jean and I found our "sea legs." That means, we learned how to walk while the ship went up and down and rolled from side to side. It reminded me of Dad when he'd had a nip of gin.

We spent the day exploring, then came back to test our bunks and sniff the air, trying to figure out what we'd be getting to eat. Our cabin is near the kitchen and we could smell the cooking through the walls, but we couldn't make out what the food *was*. When we went into the dining room we discovered it was soup — or maybe stew. It looked rather grayish. Nothing that Mrs. Angel would be proud to serve, that's certain.

And nothing that Alice could keep down. Alice ate half of her meal, then put her hand to her mouth and looked at us in alarm. "What's wrong?" I asked. But she couldn't answer. She fled from the table, back to our room and the bucket. When I went to find her, she was a strange greenish colour and lay moaning on her bunk. Poor Alice. Jean and Amy and Miss Dorgan and I brought her a bit of soup and some tea and emptied out her throwing up bucket, but she just moaned and slept.

That first afternoon, Miss Dorgan gathered up all the Home Girls in our cabin so Alice could hear, and read out the rules about which deck we could go on and which deck was *forbidden*. She said we'd have prayer and singing in the dining room every night after dinner and she expected to see us all there. She said we were to keep our cabins *neat, girls, shipshape, girls.* "Shipshape" was her idea of a little joke. I felt so sorry for her I laughed a bit.

She told us a list of rules about a mile long while I sat and felt the gentle swells of the ocean waves and repeated over and over to myself, "I am on the ocean. Sailing to Canada. Land of the silver birch, home of the beaver. I, Gwen Peters, have started an adventure." That's how my dad would have thought. I could almost hear his voice. "Life is an adventure, Gwen Peters," he'd say. "Make the most of it. Don't waste your time with those inflicted with bad attitudes. You never know what's around the corner, girl, unless you take a look.

Could be that corner will change your life!"

"And if it's a dangerous lion or a man-eating giant?" I'd asked once, laughing, as we walked home together from the theatre.

"Why, then you'd have a good story to tell, wouldn't you?" And he laughed and bowed low. "May I have this dance?" he asked.

Our music was the clip-clop of a horse and carriage on the next street. We waltzed along the street until he stepped in the soggy mess in the gutter. He stopped, swore, laughed and kept on dancing.

*

The first night on the ship, I lay on my bunk thinking about Miss Pauline Johnson making a voyage like this one. Only she was going home, and I was leaving home. Or was I? Maybe Canada would become my home. I hoped so, with all my heart. And maybe Pet would come over some day and maybe Tim really would be a gentleman farmer and buy up a theatre for us. And the first play would be called, "The Adventures of Tim and Gwen Finding Home." I fell asleep to the music of throbbing engines and the creaking of the ship.

Banging just above my head woke me in the morning. It was only people walking up there, but it sounded like they might come through the ceiling and land on me. I dressed as quickly as I could, and even got a weak smile out of poor Alice as she watched me hopping about to the rolling of the ship as I tried to get my shoes on. I gave her a wink and went out with the others to see what the day had brought. I was hoping I could see some whales or big fish, but what I saw were seagulls. Lots of them, circling, crying and calling, their pure white angel wings looking eerie against the dark gray sky.

By noon, the deck of the ship wouldn't stay beneath my feet. The ship bobbed around like a little cork as the wind howled and the rain poured down sideways. We ran for our cabins and found Alice hanging over the bucket, moaning and crying. "We're going to die!" she said. "Of course we're not!" I told her, even though I thought she might be right. "But I *want* to die!" she said.

Our trunks slid first to one side and then the other. The gas lamp on the ceiling danced crazily this way and that. Everything that was not nailed down moved back and forth: a pair of shoes, a basket, a cup, a book, the vomit in the bucket. Miss Dorgan came in, no parasol in her hand this time, and said we were to stay in our cabins until she came for us. There wasn't much chance we'd disobey her. The only time any one of us got up it was to use Alice's bucket. It wasn't long before the stink in the cabin made everyone sick. How long can a storm at sea last, I wondered.

Up and down, up and down, the ship bobbed and shuddered and creaked. I thought that soon it would break into a million pieces. I thought about the girl in the *Wreck of the Hesperus* lashed to the mast in the storm. I thought about Jesus on the boat sleeping through the whole storm while the disciples went wild with fear. I thought that my adventure might be over, and that I, Gwen Peters, would turn into fish food. I lay in bed and told God how much I'd appreciate it if the boat could get to Canada with me on it. Alive. Then I asked God to look after Pet and Tim and even Mrs. Bostwick. I pulled the blanket over my head, closed my eyes and waited for the end.

Chapter Nine

BONJOUR, CANADA

THE BANGING OVERHEAD WOKE ME AGAIN. I LAY FOR A moment, listening. The ship creaked peacefully. The lamp swayed gently. The storm had ended! I got dressed and nipped to the toilet to empty the bucket. By the time I'd cleaned up the mess in our cabin, the others were awake. "The sun is shining!" I announced, "And we are alive!"

After living in the Home, sailing was a holiday. I don't know who cooked, but it wasn't me. I don't know who washed up, but it wasn't me. I don't know who mended the torn tea towels, but I didn't do it. I couldn't remember a time when I could read a book all day or stroll around or feed the seagulls bits of biscuits or do anything I wanted, within Miss Dorgan's limits, of course. It felt strange. So strange in fact, that I asked Miss Dorgan if I might have some paper and a pencil. I rewrote Mr. Longfellow's *Wreck of the Hesperus*. In my poem, the girl doesn't get lashed to the mast or end up dead. She sails that ship to safety. By herself. I tucked it inside *White Wampum* for safe keeping.

In the afternoon we saw a ship in the distance, going in the opposite direction. "Imagine if it was a pirate ship," Amy said. "Imagine if they boarded us!" And we made up a play on the spot about how they would come alongside and jump on, and we'd have to battle them with swords. And then Miss Dorgan appeared.

"Ladies do not play at pirates! I expect you to be ladies on this voyage and to conduct yourselves accordingly. *Decorum,* girls!"

So we stood at the railing like decorations and I wondered how people ever managed to live with so little imagination. As we watched the smoke from the three stacks trail out in the wind, I felt quite sorry for Miss Dorgan.

Watching the distant ship gave me an urge to wave, call, send a message. I was homesick. Straightaway I went to get paper and pencil. I sat on the deck and wrote the longest letter to Tim, telling him everything that had happened on the train rides and the ship so far. I wrote that I hoped I would see him in Canada some day. I wrote until my poor little heart felt calm and Jean came to get me for dinner.

Walking back to our cabin after prayers that night I noticed the moon, and stopped. It was full and low, and cast a silver light on the sea. That same moon shone in England on all my friends there. It shone on all the wild animals and great forests in Canada. Maybe Miss Pauline Johnson was looking at it too, conjuring up a new poem for a new book. "Don't be long," Jean said. "And don't fall overboard," Amy added as they stepped inside the cabin. I stood by the railing near the lifeboat and whispered a verse from Miss Johnson's "Moonset":

"The troubled night-bird, calling plaintively,
Wanders on restless wing;
The cedars, chanting vespers to the sea,
Await its answering,
That comes in wash of waves along the strand,
The while the moon slips into shadow-land."

Suddenly I stopped. Had something moved right beside me? I thought I was seeing things. I imagined that a shadowy form had lifted the tarp on the lifeboat.

I saw it again. Holding my breath, I glanced left and right. I was alone. When the tarp moved a third time, my stomach clenched like a fist. I stepped into the shadows against the wall. We hit a big swell; the tarp went still as the ship came to rights again.

After an eternity, after I'd decided that there was a pirate under there with a big knife that would slice my body in half with one quick swipe, a man's head appeared. He looked around, climbed up and then jumped, landing with a soft plop on the deck. No knife.

His eyes were huge. His face, under the dirt, was as white as paper. He looked familiar. I stepped out of the shadows. His fist came up fast as he whirled to face me.

"Tim?" I said. He jumped a foot in the air, I swear. "Tim?"

"Gwen?"

We stood like statues for a long moment, then he grabbed my hand pulled me along the deck and behind a bench.

"Finally! I didn't know how I was going to talk to you without anyone else seeing me." Crouching there, Tim whispered his story. When he got my farewell letter, he had decided that this would be the time to cross to Canada, too.

"Really?" I said. My voice came out like a squeak. "Gwen," he said, "you remember about the gold and the farm and the theatre, don't you? Didn't you believe me? And anyway, who would watch out for you with the bears and all?" Then we laughed and the only thing that really mattered was that he was here, now.

Tim had walked and hitched rides to Liverpool and sneaked onto the boat in a barrel. He'd been hiding in the lifeboat for four days. His food was gone. "Can you nick something to eat and drink, Gwen?" he asked.

I couldn't help it. I laughed. "So who is looking after who, did you say?" He laughed, too. "What a good play this will make," I said, forgetting to whisper. "The Stowaway."

"Shhh!" He clapped his hand over my mouth. "If they catch me they'll put me in jail and send me back."

For the next six days I put buns and bits of meat and dried fruit in my pockets whenever I could. Every night I went out on deck to "catch a little air." When I was alone I'd knock on the lifeboat three times and he'd peek out and wait impatiently while I emptied my pockets. Knowing Tim was there, I felt like I had a little of London with me after all. Tim's first plan was to go out west and find some gold and get rich and be a gentleman. Then he would send for me.

"Where *is* out west?" I asked one night.

Tim stared out at the deck for a moment, his face red. "Well," he said, "well ..."

I waited. "Tim! Where *is* it? Don't you know?"

"Of *course* I know, silly. It's ... where the sun sets. Out where there are horses and big trees and mountains. And it's where the gold just lies there in the rivers and waits for a man to pick it up. *That's* where it is."

"And is it far from Toronto?"

"Pretty far, I think," he answered.

"And will you be able to visit me?"

"Gwen! You're pestering me with too many questions. It's hard for a man to even think at all," he said.

After a week of sailing I wanted the voyage to end. The sea rolled on and on and on; it seemed endless. At first it was fun to be free of duties, but eventually, I'd had enough walking on the deck, reading and looking at the water. And I was nervous. Each day we were at sea was another day that Tim could get caught.

Finally, Miss Dorgan told us that we'd be able to see New-foundland by afternoon. We were standing by the lifeboat.

"We'll sight Newfoundland today," I hollered.

"What's wrong with you, yelling like that," Amy scolded. "I'm standing right beside you!" She laughed and tickled me. "Maybe sailing is making you strange, Gwen."

Right after lunch we saw it. Land at last! Everyone, even the seasick ones, rushed out on deck to see that beautiful rock and those great, green forests. Who would have imagined anything so marvelous, so beautiful? In the distance small fishing boats bobbed on the waves. Miss Dorgan said that cod fish from here ends up back in England on our tables. Newfoundland meant we were almost in Canada. I wanted to stay on deck the whole time to be the first to see it. I could hardly wait to land in Canada. We'd been sailing nine days.

It wasn't until the next day that Miss Dorgan told us to

pack up and be ready. I tidied my trunk and closed the lid tight. I kept out *White Wampum,* though, in case my trunk went missing. I could always make new clothes and under-wear but I'll never have another gift from Dad. I tucked it in my waistband where it would be next to me all the time.

Then I ran up on deck and let the fresh Canadian breeze kiss my face. The sea was quieter here. We were entering the St. Lawrence River.

I memorized Canada: rocks and farmland, great huge forests and villages here and there where children waved from the banks. There was so much space! I felt very small.

Suddenly I saw the water move; sleek, white giants swam just below the surface. White whales welcoming us to Canada! I had never seen such creatures; they blew water out of holes in the tops of their heads, they dipped and dove and rose up then splashed down again, like they were playing! And then, just as suddenly as they had appeared, they left us.

I looked ahead. The river became more narrow. Slowly, the ship lost steam. All at once, Miss Dorgan was there, pointing at Quebec City. First I saw only a bank and then my eyes lifted to beautiful old buildings sitting strong on top of cliffs towering over the river. Quebec was a surprise. Our ship pulled up smooth at the wharf and men fastened the huge ropes to keep us there snug. We didn't have to get into little rowboats here, but walked down a gangplank. Alice was still a little green but happy to be on deck again. "Thank God," she said, "I thought we'd never get here."

All us Home Girls lined up behind Miss Dorgan's black parasol on the deck and waited to go ashore.

Quebec City stood up a roadway, up the hill, waiting

for us. In the Canadian sun, men were building something huge that looked like a castle. Miss Dorgan said it was called Chateau Frontenac, but that we mustn't *dilly-dally*, just *hurry along girls, hurry along!*

We marched like soldiers down the gangplank. Once on the wharf I turned to look at the lifeboat. The tarp had been thrown back. Tim must have jumped out already. Two sailors stood by it, talking excitedly and pointing to the shore. They must have been able to see him from up there. *Run, Tim, run!*

In the Immigration shed we lined up to see the doctor. He looked at our eyeballs, thumped our chests, made us stick out our tongues and yelled, "Next!" Then we stood in line again while Miss Dorgan showed a bunch of papers to a man sitting at a rickety table. She said Dr. Allan's name very loud.

Outside we followed Miss Dorgan's parasol up the street that was cobbled just like streets in London and past a tall stone, rather like Cleopatra's Needle in London, that said "Wolfe" and "Montcalm" on it. "What is this?" I asked. Miss Dorgan said Wolfe and Montcalm were military leaders killed in battle. "It's the only monument I know of dedicated to both sides in a war. It's to remember a war between the English and the French," she explained. I wondered why there was a war over *here* when England and France are over *there,* but there was no time to ask because Miss Parasol was charging up the hill at a ferocious pace towards something called "The Citadel," which stood up at the top, a lookout for soldiers long ago.

As we walked up, I turned, watching for Tim. And there he was, caught like a rat! Just like that, all our hopes for the future were caught, too. After all he'd done to get here, and now they'd probably send him back. Or maybe send him to prison. I shivered. He looked very small between two big men, one on each side holding him under the arms. His feet pedalled the air. *Where were they taking him?*

I tried to signal to him, but Miss Parasol was shooing us along. Up the hill *smartly, girls,* past the giant trees and horses and carriages, past houses that opened right onto the street, past the people who spoke in another language, not English. Finally we reached the top of the hill, turned right and marched to where a sign said, "Presbyterian Church."

Inside we queued again and some church ladies, who looked English but might have been Canadian, gave us buns and let us sit down on benches. I took an extra one for Tim just in case and tucked it in my pocket. I was glad to sit down because my legs were wobbly. I still felt like I was rolling on the sea.

After a while the parson came and invited us to go upstairs to the Sanctuary to thank God for our safe voyage. So up we went. I wanted to have a talk with God about Tim, and to say a few things about how this world is fair or not fair, and to ask if please couldn't the Almighty Maker of Heaven and Earth just spare a thought for a boy with boots that have holes in them and no buttons on his shirt?

It was hard to pay much attention to what the parson was saying anyway, because of two other things. First, I thought there would be kneeling benches like the Children's Church at the Home. I automatically started to kneel, but there weren't any and I pitched forward, smacked my chin on the next pew and bit my tongue. And second, the stained glass window on my left showed Mary, the mother of Jesus, with children all around her, like she was looking after them. And for some reason looking at that made me have a lump in my throat that I couldn't swallow.

We marched back down the hill, following Miss Parasol. I couldn't see Tim anywhere.

At the train station we lined up and got counted again and there were lots of people on the platform, not like London or Liverpool, but lots. I swear they were all staring at us funny. I didn't like how they looked at us. It made me feel queer, like a spectacle. Then I saw him. Tim.

He was all mixed in with the crowd on the platform and the two men were nowhere in sight. He smiled a shaky little smile. He was filthy. He casually walked over to our line.

"What happened?" I whispered.

"I put on my best gentleman's voice and told their gracious majesties that they were likely looking for a rogue. I pointed to a boy and shouted, 'There he is!' When they turned to look …"

What a relief! Tim had learned a lot on London streets. Why had I been so afraid? "What will you do now?" I asked. "I'll stay here for a bit and get my bearings. Then I'll go west. I'll write to you at Allan's in Toronto," he said.

"Be careful, Tim," I said, and I gave him the bun I'd nicked from the church and then I started to cry and he said, "Don't do that, Gwen. We'll be alright. Never say die, right?"

I took *White Wampum* from my waistband, and I'm sure I heard Dad's voice again, *Stories will carry you through, Gwen.* I put the book into Tim's hand. "I've just about memorized all the poems in this," I said. His hand closed over mine and he looked into my eyes, serious. "I'll look after it until I see you again."

Miss Parasol hacked at the air again and called us to board the train. I hurried up the step and ran to open a window so I could lean out and see Tim one last time.

The whistle blew; the train moved. Tim held *White Wampum* to his chest with one hand and waved with the other. I watched until he was a tiny speck on the platform. Then he was gone.

The man sitting opposite said, "Dere, dere, little one. You'll see your brudder again, dat's for sure."

I didn't want to talk to anyone. I only wanted to know that Tim would be alright. I wiped my eyes and watched out the window, as the city faded away and the forests and farmlands appeared. The man said nothing more. The swaying of the train eventually calmed me; my hands were not fists anymore. I realized that mixed in with the scenery outside, I could see the old man's reflection on the glass.

He was old, with white hair, a big, big moustache and twinkly eyes. He wore an unbuttoned red and black plaid jacket made of wool. Under it, he wore a rough brown shirt and trousers held up with red suspenders. His hands were big and rough and tanned. His nails were short and square, like my dad's. He saw me watching him and winked at my reflection. I couldn't help it. I smiled back at him.

"*Bonjour, chérie.* I am Pierre Paul," he said. "Da ride to Toronto, she's a long one."

Before I could make up my mind whether to talk to the old man or not, I glanced around the car. Alice and Jean were in the seats ahead, and others from the ship were in our row further on in the car. I looked, and looked again. No Amy!

Chapter Ten

LESSONS

"Where's Amy?" I asked, scrambling into the aisle. Jean's eyes were half shut like when she's bleedin' mad. She pointed outside. Just then Miss Parasol came down the aisle with papers and a list. She nodded at me, like I should return to my seat. I didn't. She leaned over and pinned papers on Jean and Alice that said "Belleville." On me she pinned one that said, "Peterborough via Toronto."

"Where's Amy?" I asked. I felt scared.

"She stayed in Quebec. There were ..." she flipped her list "... nine girls who stayed. And there are ... let me see ... six will get off in Montreal; they go to the Eastern Townships ... and —"

I interrupted her. "But Amy was our friend!" I yelled. "We didn't even say goodbye!"

"*Calm* yourself, Missy. *Decorum at all times.* We divided up on the platform. Didn't you see?"

The train picked up speed. "But we didn't even say goodbye," I repeated. I sat down, overwhelmed. It was too much.

I didn't think it would happen like this. I thought we'd be together, at least in the same town, not like this in this great big country … not like this … I started to cry.

"There now," Miss Parasol said. "You can write to each other. You're very lucky girls, you know, *very fortunate*. You could be still in the gutters of London. In Canada you have all the opportunities in the world. Now I must go and tag the other girls. No more nonsense." And she left, steadying herself on a seatback as the train lurched around a corner.

Alice stuck out her tongue at her departing back.

"We look like legs of lamb in a bleedin' butcher shop window!" Jean said, and she ripped off her tag and threw it on the floor. Everything seemed to be moving too fast. That concert in the dining hall seemed a blur now. For a while, no one spoke, and we each sat with our own thoughts as the train swayed its way along the tracks.

After some time, Jean and Alice said they were bored and decided to explore the train. "Why don't you come?" Jean asked. "There's *nothing* to look at out the window." But I didn't feel like it. I just wanted to sit still and think about things.

The old man across from me watched them go. "Eh!" he said. "Dose girl don't know what dey look at! Dat's not *no-ting* outside. Dat's *some-ting*, for sure."

He smiled at me. "You tink I talk funny?" he asked. "Eh! I tink you talk funny, too!" And he laughed and I couldn't help it. I laughed, too.

Pierre Paul was something called a "lumberjack," and that meant he cut down trees for people to build houses and make furniture and light the fires. In winter he hauled logs out of the forest on a sled, pulled by a team of horses. I could see he was a strong man, even though he was old. His hands were big and brown and hairy. He could probably yank a whole tree out of the ground just by pulling.

"Where do you live?" I asked, hoping he'd say Toronto or some other town I'd at least heard of. But he answered, "Mostly in de lumber camps. I go to Montreal for sometimes and Quebec for sometimes, and for sometimes I'm go to my baby daughter, married to an *anglais*. She live in Brantford. I'm go dere now for she have a new baby. A boy dis time after so many girls, *mon Dieu*. So, I make de travel."

Pierre Paul said that Alice and Jean have English eyes. They cannot see what they are looking at. "Dere is never no-ting out dere, *chérie!* Dere is life!"

I looked and looked out the window and then I began to see what he meant. At first all I could see were miles and miles of trees. And then rivers, some fast, some meandering, home to families of lovely brown ducks. I noticed fir trees, dark against other trees with light green leaves. I saw a flock of black crows swoop like a cloud over treetops. My breath caught in my throat when I saw a deer raise her head in a clearing. She hesitated a moment, then bounded into the shadows. Pierre Paul meant the forest was not nothing. It is something alive.

Pierre Paul pointed out the window at some short, thin trees with gray trunks. "Sumach," he said. He pulled a bottle out of his old pack. The liquid was pink, and there was a clump of furry red berries inside. Careful not to pour out the berries, he gently poured some liquid into a tin cup and offered it to me. "Sumach," he said again. "Some nice drink, dis." It tasted sharp, refreshing, like tea with no milk or sugar, but lighter. My tongue danced.

Searching through his pack, one by one he brought out more surprises. He shared *jerky*, which is dried meat, then little dried berries he called cranberries and blueberries, and best of all, a lump of maple sugar. "Bush food, see? And dat is why," he said, "in the forest is never no-ting. Always some-ting." He closed his pack and sat back satisfied. The maple sugar sat on my tongue for a long time. It was different than anything I had ever tasted. Pierre Paul said that it was made from trees!

He pointed out the window again. "See da bulrush along de tracks dere? You pull dem up, you eat de root. Very good soup. All in de forest is meat, too, of course — rabbit, partridge, deer."

"Do all Canadians eat food like this?" I asked.

"*Mais non.* Only very lucky ones, *chérie.*" And Pierre Paul winked. "De forest give many, many gift," he said. "Shelter also. Lumber for build houses, also she give shelter right dere in de bush. See de saplings, dose skinny poplar trees? Bend dem down, cover her wid cedar, like dat *et voilà!* You got yourself a good little house for sleeping. Take da spruce branches for a mattress *et voilà!* You sleep like one *bébé* in de woods."

I looked out at the vast forest rolling past the window, tried to imagine being out there. "I think I'd get lost out there," I said

"*Chérie*, you can find your way easy. You want to know which way you go? In nighttime you want *nord*? You look at the sky and find da Big Bear. She will lead you nord. In daytime you want nord? You find dat morning sun, turn sideways like *dis* and so you go nord. *Très simple*, non?" He laughed.

I'd never met anyone like him in my life. His world was strange and wonderful and mysterious. "I think I'd be scared out there, though," I said. It all looked so very big.

"What do you do when you're scared in dat great, big English land over dere?"

"Sing, or pray." I said. "Or make up a play."

Pierre Paul smiled and slapped his knee. "OK, *d'accord!* Dat work in da forest also. But to be walk in silence," he whispered, "dat's good too. You get to know the forest, see? In silence you can hear da grouse, chickadee and robin sing. Shhhhh! Dat's when you can stand still and watch dat ol' beaver swimmin' across de pond. Yessir. *Le silence est d'or.* Silence, he is golden, too."

When Pierre Paul talked about bush life, his eyes were happy. Maybe Canada was a magic place. Maybe I, Gwen Peters, was lucky to be in it. And the play would be called, "Gwen Peters: Woman in the Canadian Woods," and people would come from miles around to see how an English girl learned to cook up some bulrushes and save the people from starving, and also how to paddle a canoe like Miss Pauline Johnson.

Alice and Jean returned and Miss Parasol brought our supper. I wasn't hungry after eating Pierre Paul's food. Instead, I went to the toilet and discovered that trying to sit on a toilet with the breeze blowing around and the tracks clickety-clacking below can be an adventure in itself. I went to talk with Alice and Jean.

They reported that the train was long and stuffy, but had many interesting looking characters on board. "I thought I was in one of your plays, Gwen," Jean said. Since leaving the Home we'd been around people of more shapes and sizes and ages than in a long time. "You are lucky to be going to the same town," I said. "I wish I was getting off with you." We promised to write each other and try our best to visit. I returned to my seat just behind them so I wouldn't start crying again. Dusk deepened to summer night. Suddenly, Pierre Paul pointed out the window, "Look dere! You see dat? She's da Nord Star! And see? She's da Big Bear, da *Ursa Major!*" And I saw.

We even saw a falling star in that great, wide sky. Pierre Paul said Mohawks believe that a falling star is a sign that someone has gone to heaven. He said he thinks it is the best luck in the wide world to see a falling star. He said that I, Gwen Peters, had brought him luck. And he shook my hand and said, "*Merci, chérie.*" I told him that Mohawks are Pauline Johnson's people. He was impressed that I knew that. I recited "The Song my Paddle Sings" and five minutes later, I was asleep.

I woke up with Pierre Paul's red and black jacket covering me and Miss Parasol standing with our breakfast in hand, swaying back and forth with the train. "Rise and greet the day, girls!" she said.

After we'd eaten and tidied up, Pierre Paul told us stories of working in the bush and asked us to tell him about the Home. Alice told him about our performance for the Prince and Princess of Wales. "Dat must 'ave been a grand ting," he said, smiling. To me, it seemed a hundred years ago that we'd waved those irons around and marched across the stage.

"It's Belleville soon," Pierre Paul said quietly, looking at my friends. "Dey will go out, non?" At once, Miss Parasol came down the aisle, followed by the train conductor. "Belleville next stop!" he cried. Alice and Jean looked at me with big eyes. "I wish you were coming with us," Jean said. Alice cried but I was brave and hugged them and promised again that we would write, just like everyone said. The train stopped. Alice and Jean got off along with ten other Home Girls and I watched through the window as they stood on the platform with Miss Parasol talking with some ladies and gentlemen. They waved.

Suddenly Miss Parasol was back, the train whistled and we were moving again.

Pierre Paul was quiet. I was quiet, too. I was thinking about all my friends. When would I see them again? And I thought about Pet, way across the ocean. The swaying of the train was like a cradle rocking and I almost wished we would never get there, that I could just ride along quietly forever.

But then the rich green farms gave way to more and more houses spread along the track. Then red-bricked factories appeared along the lakeshore — "RedPath Sugar," "Gooderham and Worts Distillery." The train slowed. "Is end of de journey," Pierre Paul said. I didn't want to say goodbye.

Suddenly Miss Parasol appeared and said it was time to *come along*. I said goodbye and he said *au revoir* and *bonne chance* and then I was standing on the platform at Union Station, Toronto and he was gone.

I lined up behind the other Home Children. It was

exciting to be here, almost at the end of the journey. We turned this way and that, trying to take in everything. This wasn't as big as London station, but it was busy with redcaps pushing luggage carts, families greeting each other. Nearby a queue of adults looked at us curiously. We waited while Miss Parasol read out her list and called our names. One by one the girls went away with a lady or gentleman. Then there were only nine of us left.

Our trunks were stowed for the night, then we were marched off the platform, out of the station and into cabs. The horses trotted up Yonge Street, busy and crowded with horses and buggies, electric streetcars, gentlemen on bicycles and ladies rushing along the sidewalk. Everyone was hurrying somewhere, it seemed.

Soon we turned onto a lovely tree-lined street and stopped at the red brick receiving house. Here, Home Children could wait for their next-day train. A friendly woman in blue stood on the porch to welcome us. After dinner and a Bible reading, the day finally ended. Upstairs, I was glad to see rows of cots in one large bedroom. I was tired.

Finally, I was in bed. In Toronto. In Canada. Miss Parasol came in to blow out the lamp. "Don't settle in," she said. "You'll be getting the early train for Peterborough tomorrow."

Early the next morning, our cab clip-clopped back down onto Yonge Street, a glorious jumble of people on bicycles, ladies pushing big blue prams, gentlemen and ladies in carriages and cabs, and people going in and out of all kinds of shops. It looked like a friendly place. I wished I could stay, but we were whisked by it all to go back to Union Station and onto the train in no time.

I, Gwen Peters, felt I could not speak another word. I wanted to sit quietly and watch this Canada roll past my window. I wanted to think. And so I let the other girls do all the talking while I watched the towns and villages come and go, and tried to imagine all the animals and plants who lived in Pierre Paul's magic forest. And again, as Ontario rushed past the window, I thought of all that had changed since Dad died. All the people and places of my life flew through my mind like book pages turned by a strong wind.

The Home in Peterborough, called Cedarbrae, was a big house on the outskirts of town with giant trees around and lawns that slope down to a ravine. This is where girls come if their placement hasn't been found yet. Some girls might stay if they need extra help in learning what Canadians expect of them. Matron was very kind. She showed us to our rooms, and after dinner and prayers for saying thank you to God for *these, your servants,* we were in bed.

The next day began a week of learning about how Canadians live. Mostly, it was like in England, except that sometimes it was hard to understand the English Canadians speak. Jumpers were "sweaters" and luncheon was "dinner." In the kitchen garden I learned that tomatoes were "tomaytoes" and the little beetles we call ladybirds are called "ladybugs" here, but they still mean good luck.

Matron questioned us and watched closely to see if we could set the table properly, knives on the right, forks on the left, *just so.* She inspected the floor after it was scrubbed to see that the smallest corners were *spotless.* Our ironing, silver polishing, dish washing, everything was examined carefully. She had to be sure that we were good enough to work for Canadians. She was satisfied, I guess, because one by one, we were sent away to work. At the end of the week, I was the last Home Girl left. When Matron said I'd been placed in Toronto, I was glad. This would be the end of the journey that began when Dad took me to see Pauline Johnson.

On my last night in Peterborough I was sent to carry a pile of old newspapers to the back shed. I'd put them in the pile beside the kindling and was about to leave when I noticed a headline: "No More Children from Britain!" I stood frozen and read on: *The recent arrest of yet another "Home Child" this week is one too many. The misguided evangelicals must stop importing criminals, degenerates and the insane who will surely rob us blind, murder us in our beds and molest our Canadian-born sons and daughters. Between 1886 and today, the Allan Home alone has imported 6,128 boys and girls from the slums and gutters of London! We have quite enough paupers and criminals without importing shiploads from Britain. When will our governments stop bringing foreign vermin into our beloved Dominion? We implore you Mr. Laurier, as the newly-elected prime minister, put an end to this practice at once! We beg of you, not one urchin more!*

What did this mean? Were we criminals? Insane? What could they be talking about? I felt afraid. And then I felt angry. And then I felt confused. Dr. Allan said they wanted us here. The people I'd met were nice. Matron was nice. *What did this mean?* I closed the door to the shed and hurried back to the house. I didn't want to be alone.

Matron herself took me to the station the next morning. "You'll do just fine, Gwen," she said. "And I'm sure you'll like Toronto." Yes, I thought, but would Toronto like *me*?

That evening, I was the only Home Girl standing on the platform at Union Station in Toronto. A man took off my trunk and set it beside me. One by one, two by two, the other passengers left. Fathers carried sleepy little children, mothers carried babies. Ladies took the arms of gentlemen. Except for some redcaps and a sweeper, I stood alone and waited.

Chapter Eleven

IN SERVICE

A MAN IN A SUIT AND BOWLER HAT WALKED QUICKLY across the platform. His footsteps echoed in the lonely train station. "You the Home Child?" he asked. "The kid from England?"

"Yessir," I said.

"You're the one, then. Come along." He signalled a redcap to carry my trunk and walked away. I had to hurry to keep up.

The cab ride gave me enough time to be nervous. The master didn't tell me his name or say a word, but he kept looking at me out of the corner of his eye. My stomach felt tight.

We stopped in front of a tall brick house. No one came out to meet us.

The master carried in my trunk, dropped it in the dim hall and left. A tall woman wearing a brown rustling dress walked slowly down the wide oak staircase, peering at me over her spectacles. "So you're the new one, eh? What do they call you?'

"I beg your pardon, madame?"

"What's your name, girl?"

"Gwen Peters, madame," I said.

"You're rather thin, Gwen Peters. I was hoping for one a little stronger than the last one. The English send us the scrawny ones, I guess." She snorted a little laugh. "Well, you'll have to do."

A boy about fifteen and a tall thin woman about a hundred came down the hall from the darkness. "This one says her name is Gwen Peters," the woman said. "This is George and this is Mrs. Richards. Mrs. Richards is the cook and you're to mind her *absolutely*. She will tell you your duties." She went into the sitting room and closed the door.

"Don't stand there gawking," said Mrs. Richards. "George, take that trunk to the attic room. Hang up your hat, girl, and be down in the kitchen in five minutes."

I followed George up the back stairs to the third floor into a crowded little room with a sloped ceiling. It contained one rickety bed with a holey cover, a small table next to it and on the other side a washstand holding a chipped basin and pitcher. George put down my trunk, leaned against the door frame and stared at me. "The other one didn't last too long," he said.

"The other what?"

"Girl," he said.

I didn't know what to say to that. Finally, I just said, "It's very hot in here," and stood on the bed to open the small, circular window.

"It won't open. It's painted shut," said George.

"But I can hardly breathe; it's stuffy."

"Leave your door open, then," he said with a smirk, and left.

I sat on the edge of the bed. It squeaked and sagged. I took a deep breath. "This is an adventure," I said out loud. "This is an adventure." But I couldn't seem to think of a title for this play. There were three hooks on the wall. On one hung a black uniform and white apron, waiting for me.

Mrs. Richards did not look like a cook at all. Cooks are meant to be jolly and plump from tasting all their baking. They are meant to have laugh wrinkles and bright red cheeks from bending over the roast beef or the steamed pudding.

They were not meant to be tall and thin with a deep voice and only frown lines on their faces. I thought she probably wasn't a very good cook. I hoped I wouldn't starve.

Mrs. Richards barked that my duties would begin at six in the morning, *in uniform*. "And if it's too big, you'll pin it." I was to stoke the fire in the wood stove *first thing*, so the master and mistress could bathe in warm water. "And you'll carry it to their room without spilling a drop, girl. Miss Marilyn," she told me, "sleeps late. You'll take her water up when she rings for it." There was a row of bells above the kitchen door, each with a sign beneath that named a different room in the house. I was to run to the room that rang. *Fast*.

She showed me the pantry *which I keep locked, don't get any ideas*, the scullery, dining room and sitting room. The sitting room was so crowded with pictures and furniture and bric-a-brac you could hardly move in it. All that curly ironwork around the fireplace would have to be dusted and washed. By me. The brass fire screen, in the shape of a peacock with its tail spread out, would have to be kept shiny. By me. All those doilies would have to be bleached, blued, starched and ironed. By me. The gas chandelier had about a million pieces of glass hanging down. Each piece would need cleaning. Just the thought of dusting and cleaning that room made me tired right out.

The next morning began at a running speed that only got faster throughout the day. I was to make the beds and clean the bedrooms and wait at table. I was in charge of cleaning up in the scullery — dishes three times a day. I was to run errands for Mrs. Richards and lay the fires and clean the grates and lamp chimneys and polish the silver and dust all six sitting room clocks that tick-tocked life away. I was to dust the figurines on the mantle and the piano and the tables and all the bleedin' pictures and paintings that hung all around the house and stood propped up on tables and shelves. The windows and the brass were to be *polished to perfection*. And there were peas to shell, beets to scrub, carrots and potatoes to peel from the kitchen garden. Once a week there was laundry and ironing. If the mending was finished by nine o'clock at night, I could go to bed.

"What about school? And church?" I asked.

"We'll see how quick you are, girl, and if there's time."

"But they said ..."

"Girl!" she snapped. "I said we'll *see*. Now attend to the duties you were hired for!" And that was the end of that.

Miss Marilyn is seventeen years old and goes to parties a lot. She sleeps late, so when she rings, I have to stop what I'm doing to carry up her breakfast on a tray and heat her bathwater. No matter what I'm doing later, if she wants a dress ironed, or her hair pins fetched, or her mirror held up so she can see the back of her head, I stop what I'm doing and go to her.

By the end of my first week, I could hardly feel the blisters on my hands and feet, hardly hear the *Hurry up, girl,* hardly see the sneering looks I got from George, hardly notice how Miss Marilyn talks to me like I'm a bad dog. I was that tired. But no matter how tired I was, the fighting always woke me up, put me on alert.

Almost every night after dinner, the master and mistress had what she called "a discussion." They argued. Their voices got louder and louder. Sometimes they threw dishes. It ended when the doors slammed, which meant they'd gone out or to bed. I was grateful that the fights were usually in the dining room. There were fewer things for them to break and for me to clean up.

One morning, I'd put away the master's shaving things, made the bed, swept the carpet and was dusting a large picture in the big bedroom. I stopped and took the time to look at the flowers in the large wooden frame. They were brown, gold and white and had little beads here and there. I pressed my face right to the glass. Could I be looking at human hair? *Flowers made of human hair?* I was staring at them so hard I didn't hear the missus come in.

"*Here* now! What do you mean by standing and gawking at my things!" I whirled around, and my feather duster caught a figurine on the table. It smashed into a million pieces. The missus flew across the room and slapped my face.

After all the fighting and breaking that she does herself,

you wouldn't think she'd miss a little blue china girl holding a blue china dog, but she was furious.

"*Clumsy! Snoop!* What are you thinking?"

"I beg your pardon, missus. I've never seen ... I didn't mean ..."

"Charles is right! You Home Children are all alike! The last one, the same. Sneaky, cheeky! And a thief, too! Clean up this instant. You'll pay for that from your wages. Once more and you'll be gone out of here, back to the gutter where you came from!"

I was too shocked to cry. I knelt and swept the china bits off the rug, into the metal dust pan, and carried it to the kitchen.

"You're all the same, you English brats," said Mrs. Richards. "They only get you 'cause you're cheap. If it was up to me, I wouldn't have nothing but Canadian-born help."

*

The thing is, when you're very, very tired, it's hard to think about escape. All you want to do is get through the day and get upstairs even if it is an oven. Just be still and be away from them all. I thought about writing my friends, but that would mean asking how to get stamps and paper and it was too much. I thought about what they told us at Cedarbrae, that an inspector would come along and see that we were alright. But when? How long would I have to wait for that?

Some nights I'd lie awake and listen to the train in the distance and dream that I was on it. Pierre Paul and I would ride all over the whole country, and he would give me maple sugar candy and tell stories that I could make into plays. When-ever the train stopped, we'd see Tim, and me and Tim would perform the plays, and maybe Pet and Amy and Jean and Alice would be in them, too, and the people would come from miles around to see us. But mostly, I was too tired to imagine. I didn't even have the energy to unpack my trunk.

After a concert at the Massey Music Hall one afternoon, the missus brought three ladies home for tea. The first one through the door had a pinched face and wore a purple hat with purple feathers. The second wore more brooches, rings and pendants than Queen Victoria herself, I think. The last one was slow and old and had a face like a nice dried apple. Her cane had a silver duck head for a handle.

When I carried the silver tray into the sitting room, Miss Feathers was speaking. "I've sent mine back," she declared, "and I'll never get another. It's a wonder I wasn't murdered in my bed!" I set down the tray and went to stand by the door, as ordered, in case I was needed.

"It's true. The money saved by hiring a Home Child is soon lost in what they steal and break!" said Mrs. Jewels. "Mark my words, they could be the ruin of us." She sipped her tea and helped herself to another pastry. "And how is yours getting on, my dear?"

"She's small," said my mistress, "and slow. On Wednesday I found her snooping in my bedroom. She broke a little fig-urine, something my dear mother gave me before she died." She sighed. "It's a trial, isn't it?"

"You *see?* I hope you punished her," said Miss Feathers.

Mrs. Duck Handle suddenly rapped her cane on the floor. "Forgive an old woman," she said, "but I don't believe that

Home Children are any worse than other children. Come, come, isn't all this talk just a bit exaggerated? Isn't it just because they're different from us that people don't like them? They are indeed lower class, and their English is hard to understand, but really, that doesn't make them criminals!"

"You're too soft. What I know is from experience and from what I read in the newspapers. *They're* all against them, my dear," replied Mrs. Jewels. "Send them back where they came from, I say."

Just then Miss Marilyn entered the room.

"Ah!" cooed Miss Feathers. "Now here's a young lady we can be proud of. How lovely your dress is!"

Miss Marilyn blushed and flapped her eyelashes. She didn't say who had stayed up half the night ironin' the bleedin' dress.

"Aren't you afraid," Miss Feathers continued, "that your Home Girl might influence, might *contaminate* your lovely daughter?"

"Oh, I know how to deal with servants," Miss Marilyn said, taking a little custard tart that I'd made that morning. "Servants aren't like us. They can't understand how things really work in our world. They need to be instructed, don't they, mother?"

"She's fortunate to be here at all, dear," her mother said.

Miss Marilyn took a second tart. "Why, I've read Mr. Dickens' stories. Goodness, she could be selling matches on a street corner in the rain or working in a ribbon factory fourteen hours a day. We've done her a *great service* by having her in our home!"

Mrs. Jewels laughed. "Yes, that's one way to look at it.

We're providing a community service by allowing them to work for us."

I couldn't bear to hear another word and left the room, pretending that I needed to bring in more sweets. My cheeks burned; my heart was broken. But what could I do? The agreement with the Home was that I stay here until I was fourteen. My wages went directly to the Home until then. I didn't have a penny to my name. I was stuck for two years more. But after that, *the Lord help us*, I'd find Tim. After that, I'd go and find Miss Pauline Johnson's real Canada. This wasn't it.

I had been there one month exactly when it happened. Saturday night. I'd just poured hot water and soap powder into the basin to wash the dishes. I hadn't had a rest all day and was looking forward to going to bed early.

Mrs. Richards was already in bed with a *nasty* headache. George had gone out to his room above the stable. Miss Marilyn was at a concert. The missus had gone to bed right after the usual Saturday night dinner fight with her husband. The master had gone out. Now he was back, standing in the scullery. Drunk.

He smelled bad. Worse than when Dad went out for a wee nip. Much worse. "You've been here a few weeks now," he said.

"Yessir."

"You haven't seen the city yet."

"No, sir."

"How about a little kiss, girl? Maybe later I could show you the city."

"No sir," I said. "I don't think that would be proper." My

heart raced. A lump clogged up my throat.

"Come on, girl. Just a little kiss." He came toward me, fumbling with his trouser buttons with one hand and reaching out for me with his other hand. Before I could think, I picked up that dishpan full of hot soapy water and threw it at him. Then I was running up the stairs as fast as I could. He followed close, cursing and yelling. I was terrified, not tired now, no, just ... no! If I went to my room, I'd be trapped! He was right behind me. I turned, put my head down and pushed with all my might. He fell backward down the stairs, hollering and grabbing for me. I dodged by him, raced for the front hall and flung myself into the night. He followed me onto the porch cursing and my feet grew wings. I heard the train whistle in the distance, turned and ran down the street toward it. I ran and ran down through the hot summer night, ran blind with tears and terror.

When at last I reached the railway I stumbled through the tall grasses to the tracks. I followed them fast away from the street lights, into the shadows. At last I plopped down in the ditch. I could hear three sounds: my heart thumping, my breath racing and the crickets chirping in the wild grasses. *Where could I go?*

Chapter Twelve

MY BEST PERFORMANCE

WHAT PULLED ME UP OUT OF THE TALL DITCH GRASS AND onto my feet wasn't the whistle of the next train, it was red rage.

How dare he come after me like that. And her, how *dare* she slap my face! How *dare* she never say my name! How *dare* they say I was vermin! How *dare* they make me eat all alone. Never. Never. Never. I would never return to that house!

Even though my legs were shaking, I started to walk. No, to *march! Left-right, left-right, left-right. Step lively, girl!* My boots crunched hard against the gravel between the railway ties. I would walk back to Peterborough. I would march into Cedarbrae and tell Matron to find me another place. If it took me a week or a month or a year, I would get there, and begin again.

One by one, the lights in the houses nearby went out. The night became darker still. The only sounds were my feet hitting the railway stones, a few dogs barking in the distance and my own voice: How *dare* he? How *dare* he? How *dare* he?

I walked all night long, never stopping. By the time the pink dawn arrived, I'd left the city far behind. I climbed down the bank near a stream, scooped up the water with my hands and drank. Then I lay down under some bushes. I was exhausted of all thought and feeling. I curled up like a cat, and slept.

The sun was full in the sky when I woke up. For a moment I lay still, thinking about the master, thinking about the long walk ahead. Then I opened my eyes wide. A little red and black ladybug crawled delicately across my thumb. *Good luck!* Nearby, a black and orange butterfly rested on a purple thistle flower. A big red-headed bird tap-tap-tapped on a log by the stream. I was not alone. I was, however, hungry. I wished I could have snatched a few loaves of Mrs. Richards' bread, even though it's not as good as Mrs. Angel's or even mine. But of course, there'd been no time.

I knew it was about sixty miles back to Peterborough. How long would that take me to walk? What could I eat? If I stopped at a house to beg, they would look at my uniform and apron and ask questions. And what would they do to me if I went to a house that wanted all Home Children sent back to England? What if the Master sent the police after me? I was on my own. I wished I had some of Pierre Paul's knowledge.

I helped myself to more water and climbed the bank to the tracks again. They stretched endlessly ahead, in the straightest line God ever drew. And the title for this play would be, "Gwen Peters: Walking Woman."

Before long I saw some houses in the distance. If there was a house, there would be a garden. If I was lucky, there would be an orchard, too. It was the beginning of harvest. I would survive.

What I had to do was make myself very small and hope that the dog was friendly. I didn't think God would mind if a poor starving orphan girl nicked a few carrots and apples along the way.

There were bushes, a hay field, a fence and a bit of grass between me and the garden. I figured I'd sneak up slowly because I'd need all my wind and energy for the getaway. I walked slowly through the bit of bush by the tracks, then bent double to walk through the hay field up to the fence. It was a rail fence, like a snake, so I had to climb over it rather than squeeze through it. It would be easier if women could wear trousers, that's for sure, I thought. The moment I spotted the row of carrots, I ran for all I was worth, snatched two handfuls and was back over the fence before, sure enough, a dog started to bark and howl. I raced as fast as I could through the field and through the bush back to the tracks. Mercifully, the dog didn't bother to continue the chase.

I sat by the tracks and examined my stolen property. I had scooped eighteen carrots with one grab! I laughed out loud thinking about Mrs. Angel and all those carrots that had to be peeled *just so* and all those root hairs *snipped right off,* and how we had to peel *away* from our clean white aprons, *girls.* I rubbed the dirt off and ate the whole thing, leftover dirt, skin, root hairs and all. *Delicious!*

The first day was a long one. Every time a train went by, I hid in the ditch, and walked way, way around when I came to a town, careful not to be seen. Careful not to get too close to a dog guarding a farm.

I was accustomed to hard work, but a variety of it: bending over a laundry tub, running up and down the stairs a hundred times a day, kneeling to scrub floors, carrying the heavy market basket. But simply walking for a whole day was quite different. When evening fell, my feet were throbbing sore. I sat by the bulrushes in the ditch to take off my boots and stockings. *Hey! Pierre Paul! I'm sitting beside soup ingredients!* Too bad I don't have matches and a pot, I thought as my stomach began to rumble once more.

The blister on my right heel was awfully big. I tested it carefully with my finger. I couldn't remember from our household hints lessons if you were supposed to break it or leave it alone. I sat for a long while and dangled my feet in the cool water and the blister seemed to shrink so I decided to leave it alone and hope for the best.

There were some noisy black birds with red on their wings fluttering and flapping about in the bulrushes. They were trying to make me leave, I thought, but I was too tired to move. I sat very still and silent and made myself small. I guess they didn't mind me then, because they settled down and let me watch them, right up close, as they hopped about and sang *terrr-eee, terrr-eee,* or perched on the bulrushes snatching dragonflies from the air and gulping them down. They were glorious.

I left my boots off so my feet could rest and wondered if I could make a little sleeping house like Pierre Paul talked about. I could see saplings like he said, and cedars like he said, and so I decided to give it a try. At first I couldn't figure out how to make the top of the poplar sapling stay down, but then I thought of using a boot lace to tie it to the trunk of another tree, and made the arch. I managed to get the cedar branches by pulling down hard and tearing. They smelled wonderful. And finally, to make my bed I tore and twisted some spruce boughs. I wished I had a knife, but in the end I managed to break some free. The tree bled. The sap stuck to my hands and I couldn't get it off, but it smelled good and reminded me of Christmas at the Home.

By the time the sun set, my little house was ready. Pierre Paul was right; it was snug and cozy. I sat in my doorway and watched the stars come out. I guess my old dad followed me all the way here because when I looked at a star, it winked at me. Big Bear was there, too, just where Pierre Paul had shown me.

I lay in the deep dark for a long time, but sleep didn't come. In all my twelve years, I'd never spent a night alone. I began to shiver, not because I was cold, but because I was lonely — and scared.

Forest sounds sneaked into my little house through the cracks: the whoosh of large, beating wings, a quick rustle in the grass, an owl's hoot, a snapped branch ... a howl. My hair stood on end. A wolf to snap my bones? *O God,* I prayed, *don't let me die here all by myself. It's not your fault the Master got drunk and came after me, I'm not blaming you, but I need you now to help me stop shaking. I need you to come into my little house and make me brave.*

I reached out the doorway just far enough to pull up a couple of sticks and some tall grass across the opening, and lay down again, shivering in the inky black. I tried to sing, but my voice came out too small. And I remembered: "Sleep, with her tender balm, her touch so kind, has passed me by ..." I closed my eyes and forced my mind to see the page from *White Wampum*. Forced my mind to remember Miss Johnson's words and to picture them. I whispered them into the night:

> Sleep, with her tender balm, her touch so kind,
> Has passed me by;
> Afar I see her vesture, velvet-lined,
> Float silently;
> O! Sleep, my tired eyes have need of thee!
> Is thy sweet kiss not meant to-night for me?

I didn't know what a "vesture, velvet-lined" *was*, but I did know that Miss Pauline Johnson was longing for sleep and peace. Well, then. Maybe Miss Pauline Johnson would know how I felt, lying there longing for the morning light. It was comforting to think about her and me together not sleeping. Next thing I knew, the sun was shining through the cracks in my sleeping house. It was morning.

My blister didn't feel any better. I tried to walk in my bare feet, but my soles were too tender. I pulled some soft green stuff from the side of a tree and put it against my heel for padding. My stocking held it in place and I was away.

I walked all morning without seeing a farmhouse or town. I'd finished off the carrots from the garden. Eventually I saw a wild apple tree and gathered a dozen apples from it. I used my apron as a sack. Many of the apples were wormy, but I sorted out some good ones and left the rest on the ground before continuing on my way.

After a while I heard loud honking, and raised my eyes to the sky. A V-shaped flock of large birds with long necks was flying overhead. The sight took my breath away. There were so many birds my neck was aching by the time the last of them had passed. I thought again about how big the sky — how big this *country* is, here. But looking up once more, I saw the sky was full of low, dark clouds. Soon the wind came up and the sun disappeared altogether. It wasn't long before I felt the first big raindrops. It was getting cold. I left the tracks and went into the forest.

I searched for shelter where the rain wouldn't pound me. But brambles tore at my dress, scratched my hands and caught at my hair. As I scrambled through, dead branches beneath my feet snapped loud and sharp, like gunfire. A sudden bog sucked at my boots; the mush oozed through them and soaked through my stockings. I was panting like a frightened dog. I prayed I'd find my way out again.

Deeper in the forest where the rain couldn't penetrate the high branches, it was dark, quiet and dry. I sat on a large log and waited. The forest was different from the inside; sun and wind had no place here. It was warmer here, and I was wrapped in a fragrant feeling of safety. Mosses and tiny delicate flowers formed a carpet too inviting to resist. I pulled some grasses and made a little nest on the moss under a great, drooping scented cedar and fell asleep.

I dreamed that my dad and me were at the theatre, only I wasn't hiding in the broom closet, I was on the stage. Afterward, while the audience applauded, he said, "Gwen, this is your best performance. I'm proud of you."

When I opened my eyes, she was standing so close I could

almost touch her. I could even see her long eyelashes. I didn't move, didn't breathe.

For a long time we just looked at each other. Her large black eyes were tender. Slowly, I let out my breath. There were no others in the forest — in the world — just me and the doe. I watched mesmerized as she turned slowly, flicked her white tail, and was gone.

The feeling of wonder stayed with me, and I lay still for a long time, looking up at the trees towering over me. I didn't want to get up, didn't want to leave my dream, my dad, the deer.

I hadn't thought of Mum for a long time, but suddenly a vision of her popped into my mind. She was standing in my room at the Home, holding a Bible in her left hand. She opened it and read, "Fear not, for I am with thee! I am your God — let nothing terrify thee. I will make you strong and help thee." Then she was here with me in the forest. She raised her arms to the trees around us, turned and disappeared. In her place, a tall cedar tree. I felt safe and calm. I knew I was not alone.

Gradually, I became aware of birdsong. The rain had ended; the sun touched the tree tops. I stood, stretched and started back to the tracks. As I was leaving the forest, I noticed grapes growing wild and tangly, clinging to the bark of a large tree. I stopped to eat the sharp, thick-skinned fruit, then climbed the bank back up to the tracks and continued walking in the rain-sweet air.

Just before dark, I found a loose spike lying by the side of the tracks. It looked like a huge nail, with a head at one end and a sharp, flat point at the other. I picked it up. It would be useful when night fell, and I had to make a sleeping house again.

Sure enough, this time it was easier because I had the spike to use as a knife to cut the branches. After a meal of the leftover wild apples, I crawled inside and looked out at the dark night. By now I knew that I was far, far from the city. I must have walked a million miles. I whispered the sleep poem again, and this time, I fell asleep quickly.

It was still early morning the next day, when I glimpsed through the trees that one side of the forest gave way to a small lake. I walked down and knelt at the edge to drink. As I was about to get up, I caught sight of a creature moving in the water. He had a head as big as a small dog's and carried a branch in his mouth. He was swimming steadily and silently. The ripples fanned out on either side, showing his path. He swam to a dam, climbed up on it, spit out the stick and poked it in place with his front paws. He dove into the water again and brought up mud which he patted around the stick.

Once in London I had watched men building a wall. They were not so different from this little fellow. I laughed out loud and *slap!*, his big flat tail smacked the surface and suddenly, he was gone.

I waited and waited for him to come back up, but he was too smart for me. He had put on a show and that was the end of it. Move along, Gwen, keep walking. So I did.

*

Every day I saw something new and marvelous: birds, geese, ducks, butterflies; frogs, a golden snake, fireflies dancing in the night air. One day it was two fat porcupines high up in a big tree with long, long needles. Needles on needles, I thought. They took no notice of me, so I stood beneath that tree and watched. After a while I realized there wasn't much *to* watch. All they did was sit up there on their branches and chew. Then I thought perhaps they might enjoy watching *me*, so I sang "Joy to the World," and did a bit of a dance for them. They just kept right on chewing.

It was late afternoon on my seventh day. I was hungry, wishing I'd taken more of those tasty radishes from the last garden I'd visited. That's when I saw her. She was bigger than a horse or a cow, even sitting down. A great, brown bear. I froze. She froze. We looked at each other for a long time, then slowly she reached out her huge paw and pulled several bushes toward her. She raised them to her face and stuck out her long pink tongue, delicately searching for the prizes hidden under the leaves. All the while she was watching me. She was beautiful, sitting there like the queen of all the land, sitting there like a fat old woman all bundled up in a brown fur coat.

After what seemed like a long time, but maybe it wasn't, she released the bushes, stood up slowly and walked toward the forest. She paused, looked back at me, and then disappeared. I waited.

Finally, sure she was gone, I walked slowly over to where she had been. What was she eating?

That's when I first discovered the marvelous red, juicy, tangy taste of raspberries. They were the most delicious fruit I'd ever eaten, like red jewels. My hands were covered with juice before I figured out how to pluck them gently, as she

had. "Thank you Bear, for showing me this gift of the forest."
Pierre Paul was right. If you know how to look, she will feed
you. As I climbed back up the bank to the tracks, there was
a rustle behind me. I looked back. There was the bear, back
at the berry patch. I smiled at her.

*

When I saw the sign for Bethany, I knew that I was close
to Peterborough. Finally! I hoped with all my heart that
Matron wouldn't be angry with me for running away.

It took a long time to get to sleep that night, thinking
about what might happen in Peterborough, but I was awake
before dawn. There was something different about the air.
Something strange and sharp at the back of my throat, too.
It was something familiar, but what?

Smoke. *Fire.* I snatched away the brush and peered out
of my sleeping house. The stars looked — *not stars* — sparks
in a smoky gray and pink sky! I jumped to my feet as a giant
owl sliced the air above my head. A deer galloped past. My
heart crashed against my ribs as I strained to see through the
gray dawn, the smoky haze. The whole forest was moving,
raccoons, squirrels, groundhogs, foxes, rabbits desperate to
outrace the fire.

I stood, desperate to comprehend the approaching dis-
aster. With trembling hands I grabbed my boot lace from
the branch of my shelter, and quickly stooped and wrapped
it round my boot. More animals pelted past me, oblivious
to my presence, bent only on survival. Suddenly the roar of
the raging red and yellow inferno filled my ears. I turned in
panic and fled with the other creatures.

Chapter Thirteen

"GOOD HEAVENS!"

I WAS UP AND RUNNING, MY THROAT BURNING WITH THE smoke. I ran with the ashes blowing in the wind. I ran with the deer along the narrow tracks, with the raccoons, rabbits and foxes, away from the sparks and smoke blowing behind us. I was afraid to stop. I ran all morning. I ran until my chest heaved and my legs felt like they too were on fire. Falling, stumbling, running, my heart pounding in my ears, I ran for my life. The sky lightened slowly, and I ran on and on, ran from that devil fire.

"Dear God," I screamed, "Help! Stop the bleedin' fire!" I yelled for my dad, my mother, Mrs. Bostwick ... "Somebody, help me!" But there was no road out, and no answer, only the roar of the fire, always closer.

The sun was a bloody red ball in an angry gray sky. By the time it hung overhead, something had changed. What? I stopped running, stood heaving, and looked around me. The wind had shifted. It was blowing *at* me now, *against* the fire. Was I safe?

I stood in wonder, the blood pounding in my ears. But it was true. When I began to catch my breath I started walking. I felt unreal, light-headed. As I walked, I kept looking back to be sure the the fire had stopped chasing me. My throat still burned, but the wind now smelled fresh. For the rest of the afternoon it blew back into the fire. Eventually I couldn't smell the smoke anymore.

By the time I reached a river, I was almost breathing normally again. *Thank God and all the angels.* I was so tired and hot that I walked straight into that river, dress, apron, boots and all. I knelt and drank the clear, sparkling water. All around me was green; I was back in a normal world.

I climbed the bank again. Behind me the sky was an angry dark gray. Ahead, the sky was blue. I walked on, slowly now; my legs heavy, my feet like lead. But when I was almost ready to make my sleeping house, I saw the sign: "Peterborough."

With an extra burst of energy, I kept on. I walked through town, not caring if I was seen now, not caring about anything except walking onto the porch at Cedarbrae and through the front door.

I suppose after being outside for almost two weeks I didn't look just like myself, because when I knocked on the door, I recognized Matron but she didn't know me at all. "What is it?" she asked, keeping the door half closed.

"I beg your pardon, Matron. I'm Gwen. I've come back. The placement in Toronto didn't work out, ma'am." And then, they said, I fainted.

When I opened my eyes I was on the sofa in the parlour, a doctor and Matron bending over me. At first I didn't know where I was. When I remembered, I told them my story backwards, beginning with the fire and the animals and the sleeping houses and grapes and the bear and all of it. Neither of them said a word, they just sat in that parlour and let me talk. Once in a while Matron said, "*Good heavens*, child!" and the doctor gave me sips of flax tea sweetened with honey.

I was scared to tell them about the master. I was afraid they wouldn't believe me when I told them what the master had done. But finally I took a deep breath and the story spilled out of me. Everything. And they did believe me. Matron said, "I didn't know why the other girl ran away. She wouldn't tell me." For a while nobody said a word. Then Matron held my hand and said she would never send another child there, ever. She said I was brave for telling her what happened.

When I looked in the mirror I could see why she hadn't recognized me. My hair was terrible matted and my dress was stained with berry juice and dirt and sap and it was torn from climbing fences and trees and getting caught on brambles. Even though I'd washed my hands and face in streams and ponds, I was filthy. My feet, black as coal, were blistered and cut.

The doctor went away and Matron helped me take a bath, and even though I'm twelve years old already, it was lovely to have her strong warm hands wash my back so gently. While I sat wrapped in a towel, she made a special liniment with egg, cider vinegar and turpentine and rubbed it on my legs and arms and on my back. It smelled awful, but I felt better. After I was in my nightgown, she tenderly rubbed goose grease on my feet and wrapped them in strips of clean white cloth.

"You look like a real Canadian now, Gwen Peters," she said, "for in spite of it all, you've filled out. You're strong and healthy and brown as a berry. Apart from your feet, you're really none the worse for wear, it seems, though I don't know how you walked more than sixty miles. *Good heavens*, child."

She sat me in the kitchen and gave me anything in the world I wanted to eat. I had a feast of cold lamb and fresh bread and new potatoes and all, but the best was dessert: juicy red raspberries from the Cedarbrae garden, canned in the summer. I thought about the lovely forest bear and said a little prayer to God bless her and all the other animals running from that raging fire.

I shared the bedroom with two little girls who were fast asleep. I climbed between those clean white sheets and slept like a baby.

I woke up with a shock. Someone was staring at me. She was very small, but her smile was very big. "Gwennie!" she cried. "Wake up, Gwennie!"

I thought I was dreaming at first. Pet was dancing around in her nightdress and then *plop!* she jumped up on the bed and snuggled in with me. I was so happy I cried. Dear, dear Pet.

Matron came in to see what all the commotion was about, and when we told her we were friends from England she said, "*Good heavens*, child, your life is one adventure after another, isn't it?"

It turned out that Pet was to be adopted by a family in a town called Hamilton and that we'd get to have two whole days together before her new parents came to get her. In those two days we were never apart. I told her some of the good things that had happened to me. She told me she'd been sick in bed a long time and that she had to *stop that coughing* and *drink that tonic* all the time. She said she'd made wishes with the fairy stone every night, just like I told her. "My two front teef wiggled right out of my head one morning, see? And then I started getting better. I guess the fairy-angels needed my teef so I just left 'em there for 'em!" After that, she'd sailed with the next group of girls and here she was.

"An' Gwennie, I still gots the fairy stone in my trunk!" she said. I told her to keep it there forever, for good luck. "And when I get my trunk back, I shall keep the white Christmas stone you gave me. Then we'll both be lucky."

I hated the thought of losing Pet again, but I was glad she could get adopted and not have to go into service.

The day her parents arrived I stayed busy in the kitchen so I didn't have to look, but of course I couldn't help it. I heard the woman tell Matron that she'd been praying and hoping for a child, and that Pet was someone the angels had sent. I just couldn't stay in the kitchen and burst into the sitting room. I had to speak quickly so I could talk over the lump in my throat.

"Excuse me. I'm Gwen and Pet is like my little sister and there are a couple of things you should know about her, like for example, Pet was an actual real angel in the Christmas concert last year at the Home and she was bleedin' marvelous, really. And in real life she is like an angel, too. And please look after her. Please." And then I just stood there like a ninny and cried.

Pet hugged me. "I luff you, Gwennie."

Pet's new mother hugged me too and wiped her eyes with a handkerchief saying "There, there, dear," and her new father got busy shaking hands with Matron and asking about Pet's trunk. Pet kissed my cheek, and then, too soon, Matron and I were standing on the porch waving goodbye.

I stayed at Cedarbrae for a week and they treated me like I was made out of china or was a strange thing they'd never seen before. Matron sent a letter to Toronto and asked for my trunk. She also wrote a letter to the Home in England and in Toronto to say they were never to send any more children to that master and missus.

A letter came with my trunk saying that I was unsuitable, too small and they wanted my uniform back. Matron just shook her head. "I suppose we could send them the ashes from your uniform!" she said.

I was glad to see my trunk again. I checked the important things first. The white Christmas stone from Pet and the Bible from Dr. Allan were still there.

The next day, Matron said they'd found a new place for me in a city called Brantford. "I have checked and double-checked that this will be a suitable placement, Gwen," she said. "The family comes highly recommended." I went to sleep that night wondering about this next adventure, and wondering if I would get to go to school again. It seemed like ages since I'd heard chalk screech across slate and I'd opened my mind to Miss Mason's stories.

After breakfast the next day, Matron went with me to the train station. She slipped a note into my hand that read, "Mr. and Mrs. Matthew Brown, Brantford via Toronto."

I was grateful she hadn't pinned it on my coat like Miss Parasol did on my first train ride.

"Goodbye, Gwen," she said. "This time I'm quite sure it will work out fine. Just fine." I hoped she was right. I waved to her from the train window.

Chapter Fourteen

BRANTFORD

IT WAS UNBELIEVABLE TO TRAVEL DOWN THESE SAME TRACKS again, my fourth time. But this journey was different — I *knew* these tracks; I *knew* these trees.

The train had barely got moving when we crossed the life-giving river I'd sat in after the fire. From the train, the river seemed small; it was gone in a moment.

Soon the green gave way to gray ash and cinders. Black tree skeletons scratched the sky or lay dead on the forest floor. Nothing moved here. It was a graveyard. *Ashes to ashes. Dust to dust. Maple, Sumach, Cedar, Pine,* I prayed.

The woman sitting opposite declared, "It's hard to believe that it will ever grow back."

"Yeah. But remember your dad talking about the fire of '75? It's all green there now. He says that the ash is good for the new trees coming up." He opened his newspaper and began reading. The woman kept watching out the window, like me. The train swayed through more devastation. *Rest in peace. Ladybird, Beaver, Caterpillar, Fawn. Amen.*

"Look!" said the woman after a while. "We've reached the end. It wasn't a big fire after all." I hadn't realized that I'd been holding my breath.

Three black crows circled lazily in the blue sky, then landed at a familiar place. "That's where I saw the bear!" I blurted. As the couple looked out at the living forest, I told them quickly about the bear who showed me the raspberries. "Oh, dear. What an imagination you have! You ought to write stories, you should," the woman said laughing.

"A bear would never do that. Anyway," said the man, "This is the wrong season for raspberries. They ripen in July around here."

"But it's true!" I said. "I was walking to Peterborough along these tracks, and ..." I stopped. They were staring at me like I was daft.

"Lovely story, dear," smiled the woman. Her husband went back to reading his newspaper.

But, *the Lord help us,* I saw them all: the porcupine tree, the beaver pond, the rain place, the blister place, the gardens I'd stolen from, everything. As each scene played in my memory, even I was amazed!

At Union Station in Toronto I asked for the train to Brantford, just as Matron had explained I should. In no time at all, I was on the next train for the short ride. As the train slowly puffed into the station, I was first in line to get off. I stood on the step just behind the porter and looked out.

A tall couple waited on the platform, surrounded by people talking and laughing and playing peek-a-boo with the baby held in his mother's arms. It looked like they were having a little party. The mother had such a kind face. I stepped down onto the platform and suddenly felt shy, remembering why I was here. A bubble of panic rose in my throat as I remembered the last time I'd been sent into service.

I looked around as the group was dispersing, greeting other passengers behind me. Who was here for me? I was on pins and needles. The tall couple with their baby walked toward me. The gentleman wore brown trousers and brown suspenders with his white shirt. His wife wore a long brown skirt and white blouse. They looked rather like twins. The baby was wrapped in a pretty green blanket. A real family. I hardly dared to cross my fingers. But they were smiling. "I do hope that you are Miss Gwen?"

"Yes, sir," I said, letting out my breath with a whoosh. It was them!

"Wonderful! And we are the Browns." I giggled. Mrs. Brown smiled at me. "Welcome to Brantford, dear. We are so glad you are here. This is Joseph." She turned him to face me. "Hello, baby," I said and held out my finger. He took it and smiled at me. "Bless my soul, girls, I think this is going to work out just fine!" Mr. Brown declared. He asked a redcap to bring my trunk, and we left the station. Mrs. Brown put her arm around my shoulder just as if she had known me forever. Before I knew it, we were in the buggy riding through the wide, treelined streets of Brantford.

The Brown's house is white brick with green trim, very neat. It has a big verandah and a front garden filled with red geraniums and pink roses.

Inside, their house is different from the other houses I've seen, because it is more plain and empty, not stuffed to overflowing with furniture and bric-a-brac all over the place. But there are lots of books. "Do you like to read?" Mrs. Brown asked as we sat in the kitchen for a late snack. My heart gave a little leap.

They had a room ready for me on the second floor, next to Joseph's, with a rag rug on the floor, lacy white window curtains and a quilt made by Mrs. Brown's own mother. The quilt was like a stained glass window with velvet and silk shapes and embroidery on every patch. I was sure it would take me at least a hundred years to make one like that. It was the most beautiful room ever. Mr. Brown carried up my trunk and I unpacked while Mrs. Brown put the baby in his cradle. Then she tucked me in and said, "I hope you are happy here." I thought I'd died and gone to Heaven.

After breakfast, Mrs. Brown decided to keep me home since it was Friday and it would be nicer to start school at the beginning of the week. "Besides," she said, "we can start to get to know each other. How much do you know about babies?"

"Just that they're little," I said. She laughed. "Your baby lessons start now! You can watch me feed and change him. Then he'll have a nap and we'll make a batch of pickles. Matthew grew enough cucumbers in his garden to feed all of Brantford."

"And my duties, ma'am?" I asked.

"After school, I'd like you to help with the baby, with dinner and washing up. I'm working with women's committees so I need an extra hand around here. And maybe, once you're comfortable with the baby, you could look after him sometimes in the evenings when Matthew and I go to the Opera House or a city hall meeting. How does that sound? I think we'll grow into it all together, Gwen."

I can't believe they want me to stay here and hardly do a thing for my keep. I even get to eat meals with them, not like at the other place where I had to eat in the kitchen corner alone.

While we were scalding the jars for pickles, a bell rang. I wiped my hands and ran to open the door, but there was no one there. When I got back to the kitchen, Mrs. Brown was hooking a small trumpet-thing onto a box on the wall. She was laughing. "It's called a telephone, Gwen. It can connect to other people's telephones in houses far away and we can talk to each other like we were right here in the same room. A teacher for deaf children, Mr. Bell, invented it right here in Brantford. Matthew thinks it's terribly clever, but I still feel funny talking to someone I can't see!" I shook my head. It seemed unreal. What was very real was that we made ten jars of pickles.

After lunch Mrs. Brown let me push the pram while we strolled down Market Street. Brantford is a city, small compared to Toronto or London, but clean and pretty, with lots of space for trees and gardens. And what was nice was that Mrs. Brown said "Good afternoon" to all the neighbours we passed and introduced me. *By my name.*

We walked to Victoria Square, named for *our gracious Queen* of England and Canada. I enjoyed a long drink of water from the drinking fountain there. We admired all the trees and flowers along the little walkways. I loved the huge statue of Joseph Brant in the centre of the park. "You might like to know that the bronze for the statue came from England. They melted down cannons for it! I'd like to think we don't need cannons anymore. War is rather stupid, don't you think?"

Joseph Brant was Mohawk. "Our city is named after him," she said. "He was a hero who fought against the Americans and helped settle Brantford. When the statue was built, we had a huge celebration with hundreds of people from the reserve and town. I wasn't much older than you are. We had a big parade, lacrosse games, races, music. We buried a time capsule so our great-grandchildren will know what it was like here. Actually, that's where I met Mr. Brown."

Mrs. Brown is different from any other lady I've ever met. She laughs a lot. And I don't think she wears a corset!

"And," she said, still talking of that celebration, "Pauline Johnson wrote a poem especially for the dedication of this memorial. Now she's famous and travels all over kingdom come and ..."

"Pauline Johnson?" I cried. "Miss Pauline Johnson?"

"She's a Mohawk poet —" began Mrs. Brown.

"I know! I saw her with my dad in London!"

And we sat on a bench beside Joseph Brant and I told her all about my tenth birthday, the snoring, my holey boot and Mrs. Bostwick and the broom closet and how Miss Pauline Johnson painted Canada with words. I told her, too, that my dad gave me a copy of *White Wampum* for my next birthday, and that my friend Tim was keeping it for me now. Mrs. Brown wiped her eyes on her hankie and blew her nose.

She is a very kind lady and even a real Canadian.

She said Miss Johnson grew up at Chiefswood, on the Six Nations Reserve, ten miles from here. You could actually drive out there in a buggy, it was that close. She said Miss Johnson even went to school in Brantford. "I guess we're both admirers, Gwen."

On Saturday morning we all went to the market in front of city hall where farmers from the reserve and farms all around came to buy and sell. This market was not as noisy as English markets. We bought a bushel of apples for fifty cents and a vegetable called *corn*. It's most jolly, really, not simple like a carrot. A *cob* of corn is almost as big as your forearm and wrapped in green leaves. At the top there is hair poking up, called *silk*. I learned that you *husk* it, which means you pull off the wrapping, to get it ready for eating. Inside juicy yellow seeds cling tightly to the cob. So now I know that *this* was the inspiration for Miss Pauline Johnson's poem "At Husking Time"!

Mrs. Brown says we're going to boil up some corn for dinner and also make apple pies, apple butter and apple sauce, and give some to the Widows' Home.

After lunch Mr. Brown and I dug potatoes from his garden and put them in sacks in the root cellar. Mrs. Brown and I cleaned the pantry and sang about a hundred songs. We know lots of the same ones, even some my dad taught me. I also got to play with Joseph and to hold him with his head *just so* on my arm.

On Sunday we went to a Methodist church, which means you don't have to kneel to pray. The text for the sermon was the one about Ruth and Naomi who hiked into the wilds to

Bethlehem. I imagine that it was like hiking from Toronto to Peterborough. I hope somebody at the other end put goose grease on their poor sore feet. I thought how lucky Naomi was to have Ruth say, "Wherever you go, I will go; wherever you live, I will live. Your people will be my people, and your God will be my God." A best friend is better than being rich, I thought.

That evening, Mrs. Brown said I could choose any book from the sitting room shelf and she would read it. It was a hard choice: *Shakespeare's Poems, The Canadian Settler's Guide, The Water Babies, Treasure Island, A Child's Garden of Verses, A Social Departure, The Bible, Audubon's Birds of America* ... it was a feast of stories! I chose *Alice's Adventures in Wonderland* by Lewis Carroll.

Mr. Brown came in, with Joseph half asleep in his arms. He settled into a chair and began to rock. "You like books?" he asked.

"Yessir. My dad said that stories can carry you through," I said.

"I believe your father was a very wise man," he replied.

Mrs. Brown brought in a pair of socks, a needle, a darning egg and wool. She handed them to me. "If you mend, I'll read," she said.

"You're setting Gwen a bad example, my love," he said. "If it gets out that there's novel-reading in this household, I'll be in trouble!"

Mrs. Brown laughed. "There was a big squabble about the public library, Gwen," she said. "Some men are afraid that if women read novels they'll neglect their wifely duties. Husbands and children will starve to death!"

"Just look at me," Mr. Brown said, patting his stomach and smiling.

Mrs. Brown smiled back. "We're making progress. Women have the right to vote in New Zealand now. Maybe in your life time we'll even get the vote in Canada!" Suddenly, Joseph burped loudly. "Absolutely right, my son!" cried Mr. Brown, and we all laughed.

The fire crackled, Mr. Brown rocked and I threaded the darning needle. Mrs. Brown turned up the lamp and opened the book.

> *Alice was beginning to get very tired of sitting by her sister on the bank, and of having nothing to do. Once or twice she had peeped into the book her sister was reading, but it had no pictures or conversations in it, and what is the use of a book, thought Alice, without pictures or conversations? So she was considering in her own mind ... whether the pleasure of making a daisy chain was worth the trouble of getting up and picking the daisies, when a white rabbit with pink eyes ran close by her.*
>
> *There was nothing very remarkable in that, nor did Alice think it so very much out of the way to hear the rabbit say to itself, "Dear, dear! I shall be too late!"*

I wished with all my heart that she would keep turning the pages, but after two chapters, she closed the book. "To be continued tomorrow evening," she said. "I think it's bedtime now. She took the darning from me and held it in the light. "This is good work, Gwen. Thank you." She reached into her pocket and took out a small brown book. "Perhaps you'd like to take this up with you?" It was *White Wampum.* Holding it was like being with an old friend.

Upstairs, I reread "The Song My Paddle Sings," then tucked it under my pillow, as I had at the Home. I lay in the dark for a long while. Miss Johnson, Alice, Ruth and Naomi danced behind my eyes. Tomorrow would be my first day in school in Canada. I was nervous and excited.

My excitement didn't last five minutes after I got up. I'd grown over the summer. My school dress from England, the one I'd worked so hard on at the Home, was too short and too tight on my shoulders. "Oh dear," Mrs. Brown said. "We'll have to run over to Grant's Dressmaking Shop, or order something from Mr. Eaton. Never mind, for the first day, maybe it will be alright." But it wasn't.

When I entered the classroom, the children turned in their seats and stared. When the teacher asked my name and where I was from, they giggled when I answered. I was given a seat beside Nancy whose dress is not too tight, whose hair is perfect, and who did not say hello.

The class began with the Lord's Prayer, which I know, and the national anthem, which I do not know. It's called, "The Maple Leaf Forever." Nancy's face was pinched, like I was doing something wrong by just standing there.

At recess I stood alone in the yard. When Nancy and her friend Ellen approached, I sucked in my stomach so my dress wouldn't look so tight.

"Why do you talk like that?" Ellen asked.

"Like what?" I asked.

"Like you got marbles in your mouth." Nancy laughed.

"Don't know," I said.

"My mother says it's because you're from England. From the gutter."

"I'm *not* from the gutter!" I said. I wanted to hit her, but I didn't.

"You don't even know the national anthem," said Nancy.

"Dumb," said Ellen.

"I'm not!" I said. "I do know 'The Queen.'"

"What? You're trying to tell us you know the Queen of England! Oh, *la-de-dah!* Miss Home Child knows the Queen!"

I was mortified. "I didn't mean ... I only meant ..." but there was no use. They went away laughing.

The bell rang and I went back in, afraid to open my mouth.

The next day, and the day after, were no better. Nancy, Ellen and their little group sneered, passed looks and fell silent when I was near. For the most part, the others ignored me or looked through me, like I wasn't there at all. Even *after* I got my new dress.

At recess, I'd stand by the fence pretending I didn't care. I ate lunch alone. I spent the days hoping the teacher wouldn't ask me anything, and went over and over the words to "The Maple Leaf Forever." And the title for this play was, "Gwen Peters: Lost Among Strangers."

After school, I would rush home where it was safe. Where Joseph laughed at games of "peek-a-boo" and Mrs. Brown said, "Thanks for your help," and where *Alice* and *White Wampum* carried me to other worlds and soothed my hurt feelings.

Every night while we peeled potatoes for dinner, Mrs.

Brown asked, "And how was school today, dear? Any friends yet?"

Every night I said, "Not yet." I hated to disappoint her.

"What we need sometimes is the patience of Job and the heart of an angel. Just give it time, dear," she'd say.

She calls me that. Dear.

At recess on Friday, I was alone in the yard by the fence, wishing it was time to go home. A girl walked across the yard toward me. I got ready for more insults.

Chapter Fifteen

THANKSGIVING

THE GIRL WALKED SLOWLY, LIKE SHE WAS THINKING UP what to say. She stood in front of me and looked at the dirt at our feet. "Don't pay them no attention," she said. "Auntie says they're uncivilized." A boy joined us. "Yeah. They don't know anything," he said. At first I was too surprised to speak. Then I said, "Thank you."

"Want to play catch?" he asked, tossing a ball back and forth between his hands.

"I'm not good at it," I said.

"Then we'll teach you. Three-corner catch."

They were patient. After a while, I started to get the hang of it, and stopped being afraid of the ball. "We'll have you on the lacrosse team at the Reserve next," William said, laughing. I had no idea what he meant at first, then I remembered the Joseph Brant monument. There were lacrosse sticks on it. Mrs. Brown had said that lacrosse is a Native game that everyone around plays now.

That's how Molly and her brother saved me. They were staying with their auntie so they could go to school in town. Their uncle was off building skyscrapers in the United States.

In Canada there is a celebration called Thanksgiving. It's when the hay is ready and the apples are ripe for the harvest. It's when they give thanks to God and get a holiday from school. For my first Thanksgiving, I got a big surprise. Molly said they were going home to the Reserve. She invited me to come and stay with them.

Mrs. Brown gave me permission to go after school on Friday. She and Mr. Brown would drive out and pick me up after church on Sunday. When Friday finally arrived, Molly and William raced out of school and into their parents' arms. The father even hugged William; I'd never seen a man hug another man or a boy, only just shake hands. I stood apart, and waited.

Molly's mom looks just like her, smiley black eyes, one long black braid, and a shy smile. Their long skirts were made from the same dark blue floral print; their long-sleeved blouses were beige. The mother wore a long apron of bright yellow flowers and, like Mrs. Brown, no corset. Their dad wore dark blue striped trousers, black suspenders and a white shirt with the sleeves rolled up. They waved me over and shook my hand, then we were on the wagon, leaving the city behind.

It was a glorious autumn day perfumed with fresh hay, apples and falling leaves. Red and gold maples looked like flames against the blue sky. We passed fields of wheat, corn and bright orange pumpkins. Little forests of red sumach and ditches full of bright yellow goldenrod added to the brilliance of the day.

As we neared the Reserve, I suddenly wondered if William and Molly lived in a teepee. Before I could ask, Molly pointed at a white two-storey house overlooking the Grand River. "That's Chiefswood, where Pauline Johnson grew up," she said. As we passed, I stared hard. Which window was hers? Where had she started writing poems and stories? Which window had she looked out the night that she was longing for sleep?

We drove down to the river, right on to a ferry boat — horse, wagon and all. It was the Grand River, where Pauline Johnson paddled her canoe. Molly and William live on the other side, near Ohsweken town, in a log house where grapevines climb the verandah and red geraniums nod in the breeze. No teepee. Their dog, Ji-yeh, ran wild, happy circles around William and Molly; he was glad to have them home, too. There was a pasture for horses and cows, a big log barn, a shed, pigpen, and chickens scratching in the dirt. There was so much to see at once!

Their house is simple and plain inside, not even as full as the Browns'. But it's filled with something you can't see. Love. I could feel it.

In Molly's bedroom, she laid out her whole collection of corn husk dolls on her quilt. "My granny made most of them," she said.

"She made these out of *corn leaves?*" I exclaimed. "The *husks?*"

Molly smiled. I lay on the bed and held a delicate doll. What would it be like, I wondered, to have a room and whole family of your own, with a granny who made dolls just for you?

"*Oksa!*" her mother called, "The eggs, Molly! *Oksa!* Hurry please! As Molly grabbed a basket, her mother spoke in Mohawk and winked at me. "A surprise," she explained in English.

I'd never been inside a barn. The sun fell through the cracks and made lines across the wooden floor. Sunbeams danced in the lines.

"The surprise is in the hayloft. Hike up your skirt and follow me up the ladder!" Molly said, calling as she climbed, "Here, kitty, kitty!"

A black and white cat appeared and rubbed herself along Molly's leg. "Where are your babies, mama cat?" she asked.

Crawling carefully through the sweet-smelling hay, we found them: one like mama, another black and the last one white. I held a soft, warm, wiggly kitten against my cheek. The cat meowed loudly. "Put it back by the mama now," Molly said. We sat a moment and watched as the kittens snuggled into their mama for dinner.

The chicken coop downstairs was small, dim and warm. On one wall hung a row of wooden boxes with straw in the bottom. In each box, a chicken blinked and clucked soft questions at us. Opposite, a teeny tiny door with a ramp led out to the yard. A chicken door! A red chicken in the corner scolded us then hurried out through her door. I was in a whole new world.

Molly put her hands under the first hen and found two eggs. The chicken twisted her head around and clucked like she was muttering. Molly laughed. "Oh, cluck-cluck yourself, missus! But thanks for the eggs! Come on, Gwen, you can try the next nest."

"Will they peck me?" I asked.

"Maybe. But it doesn't hurt," Molly said, and moved on to another box.

It was warm and soft under the hen. I added two more eggs to our basket. Altogether we got twelve. At the house, we checked them for cracks, washed them gently and added them to others in the box, ready for market.

Then we were in the kitchen peeling potatoes and setting the table for what Molly's mother called "Gwen's welcome feast." And it *was* a feast, like a party. Molly's auntie and grandparents came, too. There was hardly room on the table for our plates because of all the bowls and platters of food. Molly calls her grandparents *akhsotha* and *rakhsotha*. They all speak a mixture of Mohawk and English.

After Molly's father thanked God for the food and for "sending Gwen to us," the grandfather asked William where I was from. "England, *rakhsotha*," he said. "And her family?" he asked.

"I have no family, *rakhsotha*," I answered. He didn't say anything. Grandmother said, "*Ihseks*. Eat your dinner."

After Molly, William and I washed the dishes, we carried "the slops" to the pigpen. The barn sounds at night were gentle: the soft plop of a horse hoof, pigs snuffling, cows chewing, the constant chicken-mumbling from the coop. We checked all the latches against foxes and raccoons, then stopped a moment in the yard. The sky was clear.

Big Bear and the North Star twinkled overhead. "The hunters, Gwen. Do you see them to the left of the Bear?"

I did — three bright stars in a row. My whole life had changed these two years, but the stars were always there, steady, comforting. "The stars are easier to see here than in London," I said, "because of the city lights, but I used to look up at them there, too."

We joined the adults by the fireplace. I sat on the floor and stroked Ji-yeh while he lay stretched out on his side. "Will you tell the story of the Bear, *akhsotha?*" Molly asked.

Grandmother began the long ago story about the long ago bear who frightened the farmers. As she rocked, slipping into Mohawk and gliding back to English, she told of the hunters who went into the forest after that bear.

My eyes became heavy. I lay my head on Ji-yeh's shoulder and listened with my eyes closed. Ji-yeh's breathing slowed; Grandmother's voice rose and fell with the telling.

Suddenly, I am falling, falling down through space. I land in the forest. In my dream, Ruth, Naomi and I are following a white rabbit who keeps looking at his pocket watch.

Suddenly the rabbit changes into a huge bear. It runs through the forest. Ji-yeh is there, fast on its heels. In the bear's wake, all the maple leaves change magically from green to red. We are running, breathless. We *must* catch up to that bear, but I'm so tired! Ruth stops beside me. "Come on!" she says. "I can't," I say. I'm crying. "I won't leave you," she says.

We run on and on. Suddenly, the bear reached the edge of the world. She has nowhere else to run. When Ji-yeh runs up to her, the bear turns and leaps into the sky.

Ruth, Naomi and I reach the edge, just as Ji-yeh leaps after the bear. We don't stop. Ruth and Naomi take my hands and we fly off the edge of the world, into the land of the sky people.

My eyes snapped open as Grandmother said, "Now every fall when the leaves begin to change colour, Ji-yeh, Great Bear and the three hunters dip down close to the edge of the world, just where they jumped off."

For a long moment, no one spoke. The mantle clock ticked; the rocking chairs kneaded the floor mats; a log hissed on the fire. Ji-yeh stretched.

"Good night, children," Molly's mother said. William and Molly kissed their parents, grandparents and auntie good night.

"Thank you for the story, *akhsotha*," I said.

"*Yo,*" she replied, "You're welcome."

"I thought you might live in a teepee," I said after we snuggled under the goose down quilt.

In the silence, I could feel Molly's side of the bed shaking. "Why a teepee?" she asked finally.

"Because of the picture in *White Wampum*," I replied.

"That's what Pauline Johnson saw when she travelled out west. Different nations had different ways of doing things. Our people lived in long houses." She laughed. "If you thought we lived in teepees, you were brave to come out when I invited you!"

"It's an adventure," I said. "Besides, you're my friend."

After a moment she said, "I want to know something, too."

"Ask," I said.

"All you English live in castles, right?"

I thought of the Lane and our little flat with the mattress

on the floor and the fleas and the too-weak tea. "Every bleedin' one of us, Molly. And we've all got butlers, too."

"That's what I thought." And then it was my turn to make the bed shake with laughter. We laughed ourselves to sleep.

Before dawn, I was sitting on a three-legged milking stool, trying to squeeze milk out of a cow. Molly was trying to teach me, but her instructions kept getting lost in her laughter. I never dreamed that getting a bit of milk for a bowl of porridge was so much trouble! I'd never take it for granted again. The next time I thanked God for food, I decided I'd throw in a few words to God bless the farmers, too. Molly was so good at it that when the mama cat came along, she squirted milk right into her mouth.

William harnessed the horses while we carried a crate of chickens, a box of butter, four baskets of corn and five pairs of Grandmother's beaded deerskin mitts to the wagon. Then mother and Grandmother giddy-upped to market, and Father and William went threshing at a neighbour's. Molly and I were in charge of the farm for the whole day.

We played with the kittens and threw sticks for Ji-yeh and did the chores. We gathered eggs, fed and watered the pigs and chickens. After lunch we hauled two wooden baskets and a ladder out to the orchard and gathered apples. I could write a whole poem about how good an apple smells when it is first plucked from the tree. We carried these to the root cellar, then hiked out to the pumpkin field. A flock of crows let us know we were disturbing them and scolded us the whole time. Ji-yeh barked at them, but they didn't stop.

The pumpkin patch was huge, with vines running all over the ground and bright orange peeking through the large brown and green leaves. The leaves felt like my dad's face when he forgot to shave. We walked round and round, looking for the very best ones to make into Thanksgiving Day pies. I couldn't imagine what they would taste like, since the vegetable itself looked like a ball for boys to kick. All the while, I felt like I was in a play or a dream. And the name of this play would be: "Gwen Peters: Farm Woman at Work," and people would be dazzled to think that a London girl learned to milk a cow in only one lesson. Well, maybe not.

Molly said we'd want whipped cream for the pumpkin pies. After learning how to whip cream with Mrs. Angel in England, *the Lord help us*, I got to learn how you *get* cream in Canada. After the morning milking, we'd carried the milk to a special room in the barn called the creamery, where it is cool and dark. I'd watched Molly cover the pail with a cloth to keep out the flies. The milk sat there the whole day and when we went back, the thick cream had risen and was floating on top of the milk. Molly gently skimmed it off with a spoon and collected it in a big bowl. We took that to the house to be whipped later. It seemed like magic to me.

By the time we had set the dinner table and had a stew simmering on the stove Molly said it was time for a break. She pulled a carrot out of the garden, disappeared behind the barn, and appeared a moment later *astride* a horse!

"Come on, let's go down to the river and wait for mama to come back!"

"But —" I said.

She grabbed my hand, told me to pull up my skirts and

hang on tight behind her. Holding the mane, and talking softly to the horse, she turned him and we headed for the river.

After dinner, Molly's grandmother, Molly and I made six pumpkin pies. I wouldn't have believed that you can make something that smells so delicious out of a vegetable that looks like a boy's football. Molly put all the ingredients we would need on the wooden table in the centre of the kitchen. She stoked up the wood stove, cut, seeded and boiled the pumpkin in a huge pot. At the same time, Grandmother prepared a mixture of brown sugar, fresh eggs, cinnamon and other spices I didn't recognize. "Miss Gwen, did they teach you how to make a pie crust in that English land you come from?" I pulled the large brown bowl toward me. "Mrs. Angel said I make a good crust," I answered, suddenly feeling shy. "I would like to taste an excellent English pie crust, then," she said, handing me the flour sifter. And for a while the three of us worked at our tasks, side by side with only the sounds of flour sifting and an old lady humming contentedly to the rhythm of her wooden spoon stirring round and round.

That night, lying in bed with Molly, I thought about our day. Molly could do anything, not just what ladies do. She could pitch hay, haul pails, make cornbread and scold a horse the size of a house. What couldn't she do?

"One day you'll be prime minister of Canada," I said into the darkness. "Of course, that will have to be after women can vote."

"What do you mean?" she asked.

"Voting for parliament," I said.

"Oh, that. On the Reserve, women do vote."

"You mean, for the government?"

"Sure. Women are equal here. We have Clan Mothers."

I thought about this amazing news. "Wait 'til I tell Mrs. Brown," I said. I dreamed that the ladies in Liverpool were marching to London with Molly. They were going to tell the Queen how it is for women on reserves.

After chores Sunday morning, we cleaned up and changed for church. It's the same kind of church we had at the Home, which means you kneel to pray. The church was decorated with all the beauty people could bring in from the outside: a wheat sheaf, cobs of corn, pumpkins, flowers, baskets of squash and apples. Our first hymn was:

Sing to the Lord of Harvest,
with joyful hearts and voices,
your hallelujahs raise ...

It took me a moment to realize that while Molly and William and I sang in English, half the others sang Mohawk words.

The text, from the Book of Exodus, was about gleaning the fields and widows and orphans. "God *defends* the cause of the fatherless and widow, and *loves* the stranger! Do *not* deprive the stranger or orphan of justice. Remember that you were strangers once ..."

Did the preacher know I was going to be in church? I *was* one of those orphans.

Kneeling beside my new friends, I counted my blessings. It was a long list.

Fear not, for I am with thee, I heard. Were the words spoken out loud or just inside my head?

We were just finishing the lunch dishes when Ji-yeh announced visitors in the yard. I was happy to see the Browns, but I didn't want to leave. "Please," said Molly's mother. "Have dinner with us. Please, *ihseks* with us."

Before they went into the house I dragged the Browns into the barn to see the kittens. I carried one down and held it for Joseph. He laughed with delight. "Would you be looking for a home for one of those any time soon?" Mr. Brown winked at me. "I swear I saw a mouse in the house last week."

The dinner table was covered with the most glorious feast: turkey and stuffing, cornbread, cranberries, sweet potatoes, squash, peas and potatoes and to top it all off, our pumpkin pies with whipped cream. Before we began, Grandfather stood and gave thanks. He asked a blessing on the food and each person at the table. He gave thanks for the harvest and all that had given life to put this food on the table. He talked to the Creator in English and in Mohawk for a long time. I silently gave thanks for finding Pauline Johnson's Canada.

After the laughter and talk at the table, after the adventures of the weekend were told — "You rode a horse *bareback?*" shouted Mr. Brown laughing — when the last of the pies disappeared down William's throat, Mrs. Brown asked if anyone knew where Miss Johnson was.

"Touring British Columbia, I heard," Molly's dad said.

"I'd love to see her perform again," said Mrs. Brown, "to hear her recite, 'The Song My Paddle Sings.'"

"I can say it for you," I said. We pulled our chairs to the

sitting room, and I began with all my heart:

> West wind, blow from your prairie nest,
> Blow from the mountains, blow from the west.
> The sail is idle, the sailor too;
> O! wind of the west, we wait for you.
> Blow, blow!
> I have wooed you so,
> But never a favour you bestow.
> You rock your cradle the hills between,
> But scorn to notice my white lateen.
>
> I stow the sail, unship the mast:
> I wooed you long but my wooing's past;
> My paddle will lull you into rest.
> O! drowsy wind of the drowsy west,
> Sleep, sleep,
> By your mountains steep,
> Or down where the prairie grasses sweep!
> Now fold in slumber your laggard wings,
> For soft is the song my paddle sings...
>
> And up on the hills against the sky,
> A fir tree rocking its lullaby,
> Swings, swings,
> Its emerald wings,
> Swelling the song that my paddle sings.

"*Nia:wen*," said Grandmother. "Thank you!"

I felt so happy to recite those words here, on Miss Pauline Johnson's land.

"Gwen! I almost forgot!" Mrs. Brown opened her purse. "The Home sent your mail." She handed me a packet of letters and I looked through them with a glad heart. Right on top was one in Grade 1 writing, from Pet. There was one from Mrs. Ward and another from Amy, and even a small one from Mrs. Bostwick. The last one was nice and fat, and my heart gave an extra little happy jump at the sight of Tim's neat rounded writing.

"Who *are* all those people?" Molly asked.

Where could I start? The dog stretched, yawned and rolled over. Grandmother stopped rocking and poured another cup of tea. "It's early," she said. "We've got all night for a story."

"Dad's snoring was the first thing I heard on my tenth birthday," I began.

Usually he sounds like a cart rumbling down the cobbles, but this day his snoring was soft as an old tom's purr.

I dressed quickly and took money from the tea caddie on the shelf. Closing the door ever so quietly, I tiptoed down-stairs and went out into the early morning fog. At the shops I bought two buns and some new tea. The other tea was so worn out I could hardly taste it ...

THE END

Other Great Sumach Young Adult Books

Find out more at www.sumachpress.com